MURDER AND
COMPANY

uc

18/27

MURDER AND COMPANY

Edited by

Harriet Ayres

LONDON   SYDNEY   WELLINGTON

First published by Pandora Press, an imprint of the Trade Division of
Unwin Hyman, in 1988.

© Joyce Begg 1988, © Liza Cody 1988, © Cathy Ace 1988, © Antonia
Fraser 1984, © Sarah Bartlett 1988, © Celia Fremlin 1987, © Zeba
Kalim 1988, © Paula Gosling 1983, © T. N. Tran 1988, © Joan Smith
1988, © Chris Watt 1988.

PANDORA PRESS
Unwin Hyman Limited
15/17 Broadwick Street, London W1V 1FP

Allen & Unwin Australia Pty Ltd
P.O. Box 764, 8 Napier Street, North Sydney, NSW 2060

Allen & Unwin NZ Ltd (in association with the Port Nicholson Press)
60 Cambridge Terrace, Wellington, New Zealand

ISBN 044403119

Typeset in 10 on 11½ point Sabon by
Computape (Pickering) Ltd, Pickering, N. Yorkshire
and printed in Great Britain by Cox and Wyman Ltd, Reading

Contents

Foreword

With the *Company* magazine/Pandora Press 'Murder and be Published' competition, we were looking for the writers to follow in the footsteps of the great women crime writers who have made a Golden Age of crime fiction.

We asked competitors to write a short story in a contemporary setting on a theme of murder, featuring a strong central female character who can be on either side of the law.

The best half-dozen of those stories, selected from an impressive short list, are in this collection.

To keep them '*Company*', we invited top women crime writers to complete this murderous collection.

Harriet Ayres

THE REUNION

JOYCE BEGG

Joyce Begg was born in Scotland and is a graduate in English Language and Literature. She has been a freelance writer for about eight years, and has had articles and short stories published in a variety of newspapers and magazines, and broadcast by the BBC. Her work has appeared in an anthology of Scottish women writers, and in a collection of bedtime stories for young children. She is a housewife, with two student sons, and lives with her husband in a Stirlingshire village. The Reunion was judged the Winner of the *Company*/Pandora 'Murder and be Published' competition.

Sarah had never gone in for reunions, even one as small as this. They smacked of self-indulgence, of emotion recollected, and this time, she was sure, of morbid curiosity. She was used to that, of course. Over the last months, she had experienced a great sympathy for celebrities, whose every sneeze was the subject of public wonder and whose most intimate secrets the subject of tabloid speculation. She had become one of them, in a fashion. That was why she had been invited.

'There'll only be the five of us,' Eleanor had said. 'Just like the old days.'

'Oh yes,' she had replied, unconvinced. How could it possibly be like the old days? They hadn't seen each other for ten years. She was sure she had changed, even if the others hadn't. She had certainly been overtaken by events, large events.

'Come to my place, about seven. That'll give us a good long evening to natter.'

'My place' turned out to be a renovated seventeenth-century cottage, twenty-five miles from the town, at the end of a lane in

1

a pretty village peopled by commuters in new houses, locals whose antecedents filled the graveyard, and a colony of religious nuts who had bought over a minor stately home. As she approached the village, Sarah saw it suffused in the romance of an April dusk, an aura she instinctively distrusted even as she responded to it. The name of Eleanor's house completed her disillusion. 'Teasel Tops.' Only 'Toad Hall' had a greater resonance in the minds of small children. The cottage grew from the ground, steeped in antiquity, breathing history from every stone. It deserved a better name.

The others were all there by the time Sarah arrived. Eleanor came to the door to greet her, a glitter of excitement barely concealed by the warmth of her welcome. Sarah sighed inwardly. Was it always going to be like this? Was she always going to be known as the woman who, in spite of the jury's verdict, might – just possibly – have murdered her mother?

'Sarah, you look *wonderful*!'

Sarah smiled and returned the compliment. Eleanor did look good, if a little plump. Her hair had retained its shining copper sheen, her skin its translucence. She matched her surroundings. The house was expensively and prettily furnished, and Eleanor was expensively and prettily dressed. Not only was her husband the kind of businessman who regularly shot off to foreign parts to soothe troubled contracts in exchange for large amounts of money, but Eleanor herself earned twice as much, as the creator of Mrs Tansy of Teasel Tops, whom she would closely resemble in a few years' time. Sarah surprised herself by feeling something akin to real affection for the small, plain, clever girl who had achieved such unexpected early success.

'The others are here already. They're all dying to see you.'

'Oh nonsense. I bet they're all reminiscing like mad.' Sarah shrugged off her jacket and handed it to her hostess. 'How are they looking?'

'Pretty good. Not as good as you, though. Honestly, Sarah, you're so *elegant*. So tall and dark and *slim*, damn you. I feel like a cottage loaf beside you.'

Sarah laughed. 'Nonsense,' she said again.

Three heads turned towards them as Eleanor ushered her into the sitting-room. The 'look' was there, in all of them.

Curiosity, fascination, slight unease, in varying combinations. She breathed slowly, smiled slowly. Her voice was a steady mellow contralto. 'Hello, gang.'

There was no doubt about it, ten years did make a difference. Although they were still in their twenties, the finest of lines were beginning to appear round the eyes.

'First things first,' said Eleanor, after greetings had been exchanged, rather too fulsomely. 'What's your poison, Sarah? Still on the illicit Martini and Irn Bru, or have you graduated to something less nauseating?'

'I thought it was vodka and raspberry cordial,' said Di. 'I'm sure my mother thought I was a total innocent, poor woman.'

'Definitely Irn Bru,' said Frances. 'I actually preferred it on its own, but didn't have the nerve to admit it.'

Jill giggled. 'Silly cow.'

'Gin, please,' said Sarah, and sat back in the chintz chair set aside for her. The room was furnished with exquisite taste, from the discreet antiques to the rich carpeting, each item demonstrating unusual wealth. A log fire burned in the ancient fireplace, the light glancing off polished oak and burnished silver.

There was an awkward silence in the room. One topic dominated their thoughts, and no one felt able to mention it. Sarah smiled, and then spoke. 'And what have you all been up to? I've heard snippets, of course, over the years, but I've been away so much.'

It was one of Sarah's great regrets that she had come back from France. She had had a first-rate job in Paris for six years, before allowing herself to be driven home by an unrequited love affair and a mistaken notion of where to run to for comfort. Roots only remained roots if they were nurtured. Her parents, although glad enough to see her, had developed a perfectly good life-style together, one which did not include their daughter. If she had not come home, she would not have found that out. If she had not come home, the accident which killed her father and half crippled her mother would not have taken place. If she had not come home she would not have been trapped into a second-rate job in a second-rate town, looking after the mother who had made it quite clear that of the two of them, Sarah and her father, she would much rather have lost Sarah. As a penance for surviving, she had given up her freedom, bought herself a small flat near to her mother, from where she performed her filial duties. She could not have borne to live in the same house as her mother. Things were bad enough between them even at one remove. The prosecution had made a lot of that.

'I expect you're all married with a couple of children,' she said, smiling. She noticed the usual fond sort of expression which habitually overtook the features of mothers, even as they reviled their offspring. The only one on whom it didn't register was Di, who sat tight-lipped, her arms folded across a skinny rib-cage under a surprisingly generous chest. 'Tell me all. Eleanor, where are your children? Safely tucked up in bed?'

'Oh no.' Eleanor's laugh sounded faintly metallic. 'Nanny's taken them away for the weekend. She does that quite a lot, actually. I think it's the seaside this time. I hardly ever see them.'

'But how can you bear it!' Frances burst in with unexpected fervour. It was too soon to be passionate, thought Sarah. Everyone was still pussyfooting around.

'Perfectly easily,' said Eleanor. 'I would never be able to work as well as I do with kids around the place all the time.'

'But I would have thought,' said Sarah in the same pleasant tones, 'that children would be a huge asset to someone writing specifically for youngsters. Research sources immediately to hand, as it were.'

'I don't understand', Frances persisted, 'how anyone can go through all the hassle of having babies and then give them away to someone else to rear. I know I couldn't bear it.'

'Careful, Fran,' said Jill. 'You're in danger of slipping into your Mother Earth routine.'

'Oh. Am I? Sorry.' Frances smiled apologetically, and Sarah realised that although she hadn't seen the others for ten years, some of them had kept up with each other. She turned to Frances.

'How many children do you have, Frances?'

'Three so far.' She glowed with the kind of fulfilment that Eleanor had shown no signs of. Frances was fair to mousey-haired, with a bland freckled face, and a permanently happy expression. It used to irritate Sarah that Frances was continually contented, had in fact to manufacture complaints to be one of an adolescent gang exchanging grievances. It was quite appealing really. She was just the same. Happy, and stuck with it.

'Fran is one of those women', said Jill, 'who will whip up her sweater in a crowded restaurant, let down the flap on her maternity bra, and suckle her young.'

'No I won't.'

'Yes you will.'

'Well. It's perfectly natural.'

'Not to me, it's not,' said Di, still hugging her chest in the corner.

'Do you have a family, Di?' Sarah asked.

'No.'

There was a short silence.

'Neither do I,' said Sarah. 'Or a husband. I prefer it that way.'

The silence became strained as Di reached for a pack of cigarettes, shook one out and lit it. Eleanor rushed to find an ashtray, and Jill and Frances both spoke at once. Sarah looked meditatively at Di. Hadn't she heard of a romance gone wrong, a marriage on the rebound, and a subsequent divorce? There was another fragment of information on the edge of her mind, but she couldn't immediately recall it. Di was the one who had changed most. She had always been a shining blonde, skinny and lively, full of an electric sort of vitality. Now she looked nervous and taut, her hair a harsh, unlikely yellow, the energy that had made her lethal on the hockey field directed somehow inward.

Sarah's gaze moved along to Jill. It had always surprised her that Jill and Frances had been such friends at school, and still appeared to be on intimate terms. Perhaps it was that Frances was the only one prepared to put up with Jill's moodiness and ill nature. Sarah looked at her now. She had the same lank, dark hair, the same sallow complexion. She should have had small close-set eyes and narrow lips, and managed to create the impression that that was exactly what her features were like, although in fact her eyes were normally spaced and her mouth wide. She had always been mean and sullen, and Sarah had the depressing feeling that nothing had changed.

'How about you, Jill? I bet you got a first and a glittering career.'

'Dead brainy,' Frances enthused, and Sarah cast her an amused glance. 'She got a first and a PhD and God knows what else, and gave it all up for the delights of domesticity. She won't tell you herself because she underrates him shockingly, but Bill is an absolute poppet and the boys are – well – they're – '

Jill laughed drily. 'Even you can't think of anything good to say about them, Fran.' She turned to Sarah. 'They're just boys. Perfectly ordinary boys. They don't shine at anything, and show no signs of developing either brain or beauty.'

'Jill! That's unfair! They're super kids!'

'They're just *there* rather too much of the time. I think Eleanor has the right idea. I wish I could afford a Nanny.' Jill looked around her in Eleanor's expensively appointed sitting room, as though there were a lot more things she wished she could afford. The eyes narrowed, and the lips tightened.

'Jill and Bill,' said Eleanor, with the metallic tinkly laugh. 'I never thought of that before.'

Fran grinned. 'It's a giggle, isn't it?' and the others laughed, caught up in her adolescent humour.

'I once knew a Ken and Gwen,' said Di unexpectedly, and the giggling trebled. Sarah felt herself becoming infected, suddenly shedding years.

'I bet your man is Dan, Fran,' she said.

The laughter was out of all proportion to the wit, and set the tone for the next hour. It carried them right through to Eleanor's elegant buffet supper, served in the wood-panelled dining room on a refectory table set with silver and crystal and the kind of lace-embroidered linen that cost several pounds per square inch and took four hours to iron. As a display of wealth one would not have called the dining-room vulgar, but the quality of every item bespoke the kind of money that could be made by hitting the children's fiction market exactly right. The Teasel Tops characters, especially Mrs Tansy, were omni-present, in soft toys, bed linen, curtains, dress material, right down to table mats and pencil sharpeners. And all that on top of the television series. The royalties must be staggering. Even through the giggling, Sarah was aware of Eleanor's complacency and Jill's seething envy.

They sat haphazardly at the table, enjoying the perfect mushroom and prawn vol-au-vents, wafer-thin slices of ham wrapped round asparagus tips, salads full of unlikely ingredients and unexpected flavours. The quantities were delicate, the variety endless. Champagne bubbled in tall glasses, pyramids of out-of-season fruits glistened under a spun-sugar frosting.

'Makes you yearn for school dinners, doesn't it?' said Di drily.

'It's absolutely fantastic, Eleanor,' said Frances. 'You are clever. But then you always were.'

Eleanor did not disclaim her culinary talents, although even Frances had spotted the hallmark of a professional cordon bleu caterer.

'Nonsense. I'm no smarter than the rest of you. Certainly not Jill.'

Jill smiled tightly. 'There's not much money to be made out of high energy physics.'

'Whether there is or not, Jill, you chose not to make it. You chose marriage and a family. And surely the compensations are overwhelming?'

Jill looked distinctly underwhelmed, and Sarah wondered just how awful her sons were.

'You seem to have managed a family *and* a career, Eleanor, and I think it's just fantastic. Wonderful, really.' Frances spoke through a mouthful of the kind of pastry that floats away of its own volition. 'My kids love your books. I would tell them that I am intimately acquainted with the author except that they believe every single word on the page. They wouldn't understand what an author was. Especially Dominic. Sweet, but dim.'

'I'm glad they like them,' said Eleanor, unsurprised.

Frances swallowed, and sighed. 'I'm not complaining, or anything, because really I'm perfectly happy and wouldn't swap John and the kids for anything, but you do seem to have everything the heart could desire, somehow.'

Eleanor inclined her head graciously, and poured more wine. 'I've certainly been very fortunate. Writing isn't easy, whatever people think, but yes, I have been lucky.'

'Very,' said Di, looking at her plate. 'You got everything. Everything.'

There was another awkward pause, and again Sarah tried to remember the detail about Di that had eluded her. Then she got it. Tim, Eleanor's husband. No wonder Di sounded bitter. The wonder was that she was here at all. For hadn't Eleanor stolen Di's fiancé? Yes, that was it. Why, then, was Di subjecting herself to an evening in her home? Di looked up and caught her gazing at her, and Sarah smiled awkwardly. Di's expression became speculative; changed from bitter to inquisitive. The 'look' was back again, and Sarah's smile faded. In her imagination she saw, as she had seen so often, her mother's body on the bathroom floor, and the shower rail she had tried to reach to hang her clothes to air them – two skirts and a winter coat recently returned from the dry cleaners. She saw the china basin on which her mother had cracked her head when her fragile legs betrayed her and brought her crashing to the floor. She saw the winter coat, a severely tailored herringbone tweed, landing softly on top of her, smothering her in toxic fumes. Murder, said the prosecution. Accident, said Sarah. No alibi, said the prosecution. Being at home alone was certainly no alibi, but then she had had no idea she was going to need one. Murder, said the prosecution. Unprovable, said the jury. Acquitted.

Di was still watching her, and Sarah turned away.

'I wouldn't like to pay your insurance premiums,' Jill was saying. 'Don't you get nervous with all this stuff?' Her waving hand took in the delicate china, the ancient table, the Georgian coffee pot.

'Yes, I do a bit,' Eleanor admitted. 'I'm manic about locking doors, and every window has a catch, even upstairs. But it's a small price to pay. I do love beautiful things.'

'Yes, you do, don't you?' Di smiled grimly at the photo on the sideboard. The subject was dark-haired, brown-eyed, clean-featured, with an expression of great intelligence and even humour. He was indeed a thing of beauty, and it just had to be Tim. Sarah felt an unexpected pull of sympathy for Di. He had been a glittering prize, and he had been hers.

The shocked silence went on and on. Jill's mouth turned down at the corners, half horrified, half amused. Frances' mouth dropped open, revealing a chewed strawberry. Eleanor flushed slowly from her eighteen-carat gold necklace upwards.

Sarah watched her discomfiture with some interest, and then said, 'Don't you have a picture of your children, Eleanor? I'd love to see them.'

Eleanor shot her a look of gratitude, and leapt to her feet. 'Yes, of course.'

Amazingly, the evening recovered. It staggered about a bit, while everyone talked too much, especially Frances, and then Jill offered to help with the washing-up.

'Oh no. There's no need for that,' said Eleanor. 'I'll put away the food later, and – '

'Pop everything into the dishwasher, I expect.'

Even Frances smiled at that. 'Not that kind of china, kid.'

'Besides,' said Di, 'it'll give Mrs Mop something to do in the morning, won't it?'

Eleanor took in a deep breath. 'I do need help in the mornings, Di. I work five hours before lunch.'

'Of course you do. And you're absolutely right.'

Eleanor led the way back to the sitting-room, covering her annoyance and embarrassment by heaping more logs on to the fire. 'Damn. I forgot to fill the basket. Tim left me plenty by the back door, but I forgot to bring them through.'

'There's enough there,' soothed Sarah. 'Don't fret, Eleanor. Everything's fine.'

And again Eleanor glanced gratefully in her direction.

It was interesting to track her own emotions with regard to Eleanor, to stand back and take an objective look at them. The old affection was still there, but by now, after all those years, it was compounded with other things, other experiences which had altered her own personality, not always for the better. She had become more defensive, less forgiving.

The conversation returned to its nostalgic tone, considered safest all round. Forgotten names were dredged from the past, forgotten conflicts, old romances. They had attended a co-educational school, so that the memories of callow youths and primitive sexual encounters were dragged into the light.

'Have you *seen* Brian Farrow? Considering his acne problem, he's turned out amazingly dishy.'

'And Dave Spenser's a university lecturer. That surprised me, I must admit. I won't tell you where I thought he kept his brains.'

'Hutchison Baxter's on his second wife. Did you know that, Fran? He should have stayed with you. He'd have done much better for himself.'

'I'd forgotten your romance with Hutch, Fran. Was that the one you wrote the famous letter to?'

Frances' chin came up. 'You mean the love letter Eleanor stole and showed to the whole sixth-form common room?' She laughed at the memory, but even after all those years and in spite of her successful marriage, the hurt was still at the back of her eyes. Sarah turned quickly to Eleanor, who had closed her eyes and screwed up her nose.

'How could you, Eleanor?' she smiled, with narrowed eyes.

'I don't know. It seemed a good idea at the time. It was just a prank.'

'You could have damaged her for life,' said Di, unable to keep the acid out of her voice.

'Well, I didn't,' said Eleanor comfortably. 'Fran is a perfect example of Fulfilled Woman. Besides, it was all a hundred years ago. Who would like another drink?'

Jill leaned forward, her elbows on her knees. 'I used to fancy Alan Partridge something rotten.'

This was greeted by screams of hilarity, during which the said Partridge was reviled as a non-starter, mainly due to his excessively pale skin, thin chest, and the fact that his voice still hadn't made up its mind at seventeen.

'I was sorry for him!' Jill cried defensively, and then laughed against herself.

'Who did you secretly lust after, Sarah?' asked Eleanor.

Sarah stared at her. 'I can't remember.'

'Well, plenty of them fancied you,' said Frances generously. 'Old Man Martin for a start. "That's not how to hold a pipette, Sarah. Come, let me demonstrate." Old satyr.'

'He can't really have been old, you know,' said Di. 'He was probably only thirty-five.'

'God. Really?'

'The one who fancied Sarah', said Jill slowly, 'was Miss Pinkerton. Wasn't it, Sarah? You were her absolute favourite. I wonder how you stood it. She was all over you. I'd have *died* if she'd been as sickly to me.'

Sarah's voice was deep and gentle. 'She was a nice woman,

10

really. A bit lonely and sentimental, but she meant well. *She* never harmed me.' She flicked her eyes towards Eleanor, who was smiling secretively to herself.

'Is old Gardner still alive?'

'Frances, don't be silly,' said Di. 'Of course she's still alive. She's only just retired.'

'Poisonous woman,' said Jill. 'Sarcasm an art form. Come unto me and be humiliated. You're surely not going to defend her too?'

'Oh no.' Sarah shook her head.

'She had a warped mind,' said Frances. 'Maybe she couldn't help it.'

'You have too much capacity for charity,' said Jill impatiently. 'Of course she could help it. She *enjoyed* it.'

Di looked thoughtful. 'Maybe she is dead. Maybe somebody murdered her. I'm sure that would surprise no one.'

It was then that the dominant issue in everyone's mind, the focal point of the reunion, came to the fore, and stopped their mouths. The ghastly silence went on and on. The only one who was at all comfortable with it was Sarah, whose experience of ghastly silences had made her expert in handling them. Sometimes she managed to joke, or otherwise put people at their ease. Sometimes she affected a quiet heroism that shamed them and made them rush to protect her. This time she let them sweat.

It was fully two minutes before Eleanor leaned forward in her chair and spoke, with a sincerity that wouldn't quite meet Sarah's eye.

'It's silly not to mention it, because we all followed the case in the paper, and we just felt so dreadfully sorry at your having to go through all that.'

Sarah smiled. Her own calmness on these occasions still surprised her. 'Well, it's good of you to say so, though actually, of course, your support was not offered when I could have used it. Frances was the only one of all my old school buddies who bothered to write.' She turned to Frances, who had gone pink and was studying the floor. 'I really appreciated your letter, Frances. I'm sorry I didn't reply. I just found it too difficult.'

'You weren't supposed to, honestly, Sarah. It was just to say – you know – '

'Yes, I do know, and thank you.' She looked at the others. 'As for the rest of you, I know perfectly well you still can't make up your minds whether or not I killed my mother.'

There was a horrified outcry.

Sarah laughed. 'Don't be so scandalised. People do kill their parents. And their children. And their siblings. I could quote you lots of statistics.'

'Yes, but you didn't,' said Frances hotly. 'And it's dreadful that you feel we might doubt you.'

'Well, thank you for your vote of confidence.'

After that there was a succession of questions, on topics varying from how it felt to be arrested, to the state of the nation's prisons; from the behaviour of the police, to whether or not she thought the law was an ass. Their defence of her was absolute, though she knew with a cool certainty that it would not have held up if she had been convicted. There would have been no letters to Westminster, no Save Sarah Sim demonstrations. It was expedient for them now to attest her innocence, but she knew all about their reservations. Later, when she excused herself from the room, she heard the hum of voices continue their discussion in her absence, particularly Eleanor's smug complacent tones, which made her smile. For all she had answered their questions, and they would go home filled with self-righteousness and self-importance to spread the word, they knew nothing of her deepest feelings, nothing of her anguish or her fears.

It was ten o'clock the following day that Sarah heard the news about Eleanor. The announcer himself was thunderstruck, as though he was going to have a hard time explaining to his own offspring why there would be no more Mrs Tansy stories, no more tales from Teasel Tops. The report was formally worded – there was a mention of head injuries – but reading between the lines, the great British Public could tell that their very favourite writer of children's stories had met an untimely and brutal end, had in fact had her head bashed in. Standing by her kitchen sink, Sarah found her eyes seeking out the radio, as though if she didn't watch she might miss something of great import, like who had killed her.

Shortly afterwards, Frances phoned, beside herself with panic and outrage, as well as grief for Eleanor.

'The police will be here soon, I know they will. They'll think it was me!'

'Frances, for heaven's sake, calm down. It was obviously someone caught trying to burgle the place. Why on earth should anyone suspect you?'

Frances hiccupped. 'Because I was the last to leave. Last night.'

'Ah.'

'You went first, then Di and Jill, and I stayed because Eleanor was still in a chatty mood. I stayed till nearly one, and I only left then because I know John worries if I'm driving around late at night. Eleanor would have gone on chatting till dawn.' She sniffed. 'I think she's quite lonely, sometimes. Was, I mean. Was lonely. And Tim's being away so much doesn't help. Didn't. Oh God.'

Sarah noticed abstractedly how much people worried about tenses at a moment like this.

'Just the fact that you were last to leave still doesn't make you a suspect, Fran. Be reasonable. No one in their right mind would think you capable of murder.'

'They thought you were.'

Sarah paused. 'That was different. For all sorts of reasons.'

'Do you think the police will know? That we were there, I mean?'

'If they don't, they'll find out.'

'And they'll question us?'

'Oh yes. You can't expect to avoid that.'

Frances broke into fresh wails.

'Frances, for God's sake, you didn't *do* anything. Did you?'

'Of course not. I just feel – well – so sorry for her.' There was another bout of weeping, amidst which Sarah did detect a genuine grief for Eleanor herself. 'There she was, having a nice party – and – oh Sarah, it's ghastly. I do hope she didn't suffer.'

Sarah bit her tongue on the savage rejoinder. 'I hope she bloody well did.'

'Do you think – do you think it *could* have been one of us?'

Sarah paused. 'Technically, yes.'

'But *why* would anyone do it?'

'Think about it. Each one of us had a reason. It doesn't have to be a good reason. Murders are often committed for causes others would consider trivial.'

Like rejection. Like spurned affection. Like love turned to rage and allowed to fester for ten years.

'But – but Sarah!' Frances was aghast. 'You seriously believe – ?'

'No, of course I don't. I'm just saying what the police will say. That it's feasible. But not very probable. It's far more likely to be a burglary gone wrong. The place was stiff with valuables. You saw that yourself.'

'Yes.'

'So calm down. It could even have been one of those religious nuts from along the road. These types are notoriously unstable.'

'Yes. I suppose so. I wish – I just wish – '

'What?'

'That I'd stayed with her,' she said in a rush. 'I could have done. I could have phoned John and stayed with Eleanor. She was lonely, I know she was. What's the point of being rich and famous if you've no real friends?'

'What indeed.'

'Oh, I *wish* I'd stayed.'

The police came later in the day. Detective Inspector Wyllie was tall, ascetic, cold, with grey eyes and prematurely grey hair. His sergeant was younger, eager to learn at the feet of the master. Sarah's experience of policemen was encyclopedic, but she hadn't met this one before.

'I believe you spent the evening with Mrs English.'

'That's correct.'

'At what time did you leave?'

'About half past eleven, I think.'

'Were you the first to go?'

'Yes.'

'And where did you go when you left?' The grey eyes revealed nothing.

'I went home. To bed.'

'Can anyone vouch for that?'

'The neighbours might have seen me, but I doubt it. Otherwise no one.'

Here we go again, she thought, and for the next half hour she fielded all the obvious questions. The sergeant wrote her answers down.

'Would you say, Miss Sim, that Mrs English was security conscious? Did she take care to lock her doors and windows?'

'Yes, she did.'

'So a casual intruder would find it difficult to get in?'

'I imagine so. But I don't know, Inspector.'

'Of course, you don't. Tell me, did you happen to notice what kind of lock the back door had?'

She thought. 'No, I didn't.'

'Would you like me to tell you what I think happened, Miss Sim?'

'By all means, Inspector. If you want to tell me.'

'Oh, I do. I want to nail whoever did this, Miss Sim. My nieces will never forgive me if I don't pull it off.' He smiled bleakly. Sarah said nothing. 'I think that one of you ladies did it.'

'Oh? How, exactly?'

'Simple, really. If it was your friend Frances, there's no problem. She was the last to leave. If it was one of the rest of you, you made sure the back door was unlocked on the inside, which could have been done at any point in the evening, drove off in your little car, and parked it somewhere secluded. You then walked back, waited till everyone had left, and came in the door. I can only speculate on what kind of confrontation took place, if any. Maybe you just waltzed up behind Mrs English and whacked her over the head.'

'I don't care for your use of the second person, Inspector.'

'I'm sorry. I'll change to "one". One waltzed up and whacked her on the head. Does that sound better? Yes, perhaps it does. It has a kind of royal flavour to it.'

'It sounds silly,' said Sarah waspishly.

'Yes. Well. Shall I continue? I know you'll want to ask about the weapon. Terribly dull, I'm afraid. It's the old blunt instrument, probably taken away by the murderer or otherwise disposed of.'

'How?'

'Burned, Miss Sim. There was a log fire burning. Perhaps you didn't notice.'

She stared into the cold grey eyes. 'What kind of weapon burns, Inspector?'

'How about a log of wood, Miss Sim?'

'Wouldn't that leave traces on the victim?'

'Not if dropped in a polythene bag. It would leave no traces on the victim or the killer. Polythene is marvellous stuff, don't you think? It burns too. Not always entirely, of course. My officers are looking for fragments even as we speak. What do you think of my scenario so far?'

'Have you put this – scenario – to all the rest, the other guests last night?'

'Oh, of course. Their amazement at my perspicacity was very rewarding. But you haven't answered my question, Miss Sim. What do you think of my theory?'

She smiled thinly. 'It's impressive, but circumstantial. You have no proof, and so far you haven't mentioned motive.'

'Ah yes. Motive.' He leaned back in his chair and crossed his hands over his stomach. 'So far I've come up with quite a selection. Envy, for one. An oldie but a goodie. And then there's sexual jealousy – even better. And revenge for past offences. Nothing very novel. I'm afraid.'

She said nothing.

'I think it was one of those crimes committed on the spur of the moment because the occasion presented itself. Tell me, what were your own feelings for Mrs English?'

She shrugged. 'I was quite fond of her. We were close friends at school, but I haven't seen much of her since.'

'Why not?'

'I suppose our lives went in separate directions. Eleanor married and had her family, and took to writing in a big way. I worked abroad a lot of the time. These things happen.'

He nodded. 'True enough. Well, Miss Sim, thank you for talking to me.' He stood up. There was a cold intelligence behind the smiling grey eyes. 'I'll call again.'

'Will you?'

'Oh, yes.' The smile broadened. 'Oh, I think so.'

She took a fit of shaking after he left, but ten minutes later she had regained control. It was all starting again, the accusations, the harassment, the questions, the endless repeated questions.

But she would weather it. She could feel exhilaration taking over from panic as she mentally girded herself for the fight. She would take them on again, the courts, the public, the press, and she would win. After all, she was an old campaigner. She had done it before. And she would do it again. She would get away with murder.

K.K.

LIZA CODY

Although Liza Cody now lives near Bath, she was born and brought up in London. Her novels featuring Private Detective Anna Lee include *Dupe*, *Bad Company*, *Stalker*, *Head Case* and *Under Contract*. They have been published in over a dozen foreign countries.

Liza Cody is now a full-time writer but has previously worked as a graphic designer, a hair-inserter for wax works and as a painter.

Let me tell you something: on a hot day at Fantasyland life can be hell for King Kong. You have to wear long johns for the itching, and by the end of the day they're soaked. I lost pounds on sunny days. Not that it showed. A woman my size has to lose stones for it to make any real difference.

I'm not complaining. If you take all the facts into consideration I was lucky to have the job. The facts, of course, are my face and figure.

I was always going to be tall. When the accident happened I was thirteen years old and already five foot ten.

It's no handicap to be tall. There are plenty of models and basketball players over six feet. But after the accident I began to eat, for comfort really, and you can't comfort yourself to the extent I did without putting on a lot of weight.

King Kong, at the beginning, was supposed to be a man. But I got the job because I was the only one who fitted the costume. King Kong is a star. I hadn't even applied for King Kong. No, my hopes were pinned on Hettie Hamburger, one of the cafeteria troupe. But at the last moment, only a couple of days before the grand opening, they switched me with Louis.

Louis, they said, was a little too limp to make a convincing King Kong. 'All the rehearsal in the world won't turn that nancy into a plausible monster,' the artistic director said. They think just because they can't see our faces we can't hear what's said about us. But we can.

'What's that hulking great hamburger doing at the end of the line?' he said, when he came to inspect the cafeteria. 'You can't have a threatening hamburger. It'll put the kiddies off their food.'

I thought it was the end for me. If you fail as a hamburger there's not a lot of hope left. But the artistic director, thank heaven, had a little imagination. 'See if she can get into K.K.,' he said.

I could. 'Terrific,' the artistic director said. 'Dynamite. Put her by the gate for the opening. She's a natural.'

We opened very successfully with me and the Creature from the Black Lagoon welcoming the crowds. The kiddies screamed and giggled as I lolloped around growling. They wanted to stroke my fur and have their pictures taken with me.

I can't tell you how lovely this is for someone like me. Without a monster costume no one wants to take my picture at all, and the kiddies cross the road rather than come face to face with me on the pavement. I love kiddies, but I've got to be realistic. It's unlikely I'll ever have any of my own. Children are frightened by disfigurement and it's one of life's little ironies that they have only come to love me now that it's my job to frighten them. I'm a wonderful monster if I do say it myself. Who would have thought that someone like me could succeed in show business?

But it isn't like that for everyone. My friend, Cherry, for instance, used to get very depressed. 'I'm a dancer,' she used to tell me. 'A good dancer. Well, quite a good dancer. Not a bloody hot dog. It's an insult, even if I am over thirty.'

She's over forty, actually, but she's right: she's still very pretty in spite of being a little on the plump side. It's a shame to hide her in a hot dog.

'I'll give that agent of mine a piece of my mind,' she used to say, 'you see if I don't.' Well, maybe she did or maybe she didn't. The only thing I know is that two years later she's still a hot dog, and a good one at that. She says the tips are getting better all the time. She doesn't positively enjoy the job the way I did, but she doesn't complain much any more.

Performers at Fantasyland divide up quite neatly into Freaks and Food, and I think it's fair to say that of the two the Freaks are happier in their work. They are the entertainers and the extroverts.

But they are quite territorially minded too. I had a jungle, about half an acre of mixed conifers and rhododendron bushes with a climbing frame artfully disguised as creeping vines. You wouldn't catch Godzilla in my domain. He roams the area around the gift shop while the boating pool belongs to the Beast from 20,000 Fathoms.

Of course, some of the Freaks work in teams. The Tingle-Trail is a miniature railway ride which begins in the Black Forest with the Werewolves in their various stages of transformation and ends in a graveyard with a stunning display by the Zombies, the Undead and a pair of Bodysnatchers. There are twenty-three employed on the Tingle-Trail alone, and they have to work to a strict timetable.

The others give improvised performances. We all perfected the art of lurking and popping up unexpectedly. It is a delicate balance: shrieks of shock and surprise are the signs of a job well done but you don't want to scare anyone into a heart attack. There have been accidents, and we learned to watch out, especially for grandparents. The kiddies are pretty resilient; they want to be terrified. But the grandparents can be rather more fragile.

Although we rarely witnessed each other's performances, there was a lot of respect around for the way each of us coped with our working conditions. I'd say, for instance, that the Mummy had the most difficult job. The Egyptian Tomb is a maze and a maze is claustrophobic. The Mummy was one of those men who could make something out of nothing. He stayed very still, and when he moved it was almost imperceptible. It was as if he was playing Grandmother's Footsteps with his audience. He terrified his visitors slowly and subtly and I must say that of all of us he was the one I admired most.

Mummy used to sing with the Scottish Opera until asthma ruined his career. He was an enormous man, but unlike me he did not work out with weights. He didn't have to: physical strength was not part of his act. Timing was his forte. I wish I had seen him on stage – with that size and presence coupled with his sense of timing he must have been quite electric. Mummy was an artist and an outstandingly gentle person so we all felt his humiliation personally.

It happened late one June evening. The ticket office had been closed for an hour and the last visitors were trickling away. I had come down from my climbing frame and was beginning to make my way over to the dressing room when a pack of teenage boys burst out of the Egyptian Tomb and chased each other to the exit. I noticed with alarm that one of them was waving a piece of burning cloth.

Fire is something we were all trained to look out for, and my first thought was that a member of the public might be trapped in the maze. I rushed in calling for the attendant to turn on the house lights. I did not know the tomb very well and I could not waste time running around in the dark searching for a fire extinguisher.

I found Mummy on his back, his costume slashed and his feet smouldering. Smoke and shock had caused an asthma attack. He was in a bad way.

I put the fire out immediately. But it was difficult to get his headpiece off. I had to free my own hands first. My King Kong costume is not designed for dainty work and I wear huge furry gauntlets. We were in a confined space and Mummy is a big man but I managed at last. His lips were turning mauve.

An asthmatic finds it difficult to breathe lying down. I should have propped him up straight away. But his costume was stiff and bulky. Luckily an attendant arrived and together we managed to pull apart the intricate system of Velcro and zips which held it together.

Mummy was not badly hurt. His feet were scorched and that was about all. But I could not help thinking about what it must have been like for him trapped in his own tomb, imprisoned in his winding sheet.

The costume had been the provocation. Apparently the boys had wanted to unwrap Mummy. They had become angry and violent when they found they couldn't.

As I say, what we all felt most keenly was the humiliation. Nosferatu put it best. 'It's the role reversal,' he said. 'They aren't supposed to frighten us. We're supposed to frighten them.'

That made me think. 'But it's all an illusion,' I said.

'That's right, K.K.,' said Nosferatu. 'It's all in their minds that we can frighten them so they give us the power to frighten them. Once they stop playing their parts we can't play ours, and shebang! – it's all over.'

It was a conversation I kept remembering in the days that followed. A local newspaper got hold of Mummy's story and from that time on our public seemed to change.

For one thing there weren't so many little kiddies. I suppose the parents and grandparents were afraid of exposing them to hooligans. And there were definitely more hooligans. Incident followed incident. Charley, The Fly, had his wings torn off. Godzilla's tail was hacked to pieces with carpet knives. A gang of youths tried to electrocute the Bride of Frankenstein. We were being persecuted.

How strange, I thought. Because when you go back to most of the original stories we monsters only became monstrous to defend ourselves against human persecution. King Kong is a good example. Kong was only trying to defend the tiny creature he loved and that's why a lot of people leave the movie feeling sorry for him. This is because *King Kong* is not a horror film. It is a romance. Not many people understand that. But they feel it. And it was always an important aspect of my characterisation to combine King Kong's raw power with tenderness. It wasn't difficult: I think I've mentioned already that I love little kiddies.

No one could call Cherry the motherly type, but even she missed the children. 'I don't know, K,' she said. 'If I've got to be laughed at I'd rather it was the little ones than these spotty erks. They just don't know how to have a good time without hurting someone.'

How right she was. Again, it happened in the evening. They came, five of them, just as my last visitors were leaving. They had hair so short you could see the tattoos on their skulls, and their trousers were tucked into army boots.

They ran in, beating down the rhododendrons with their sticks, yelling, 'Where's the sodding monkey?'

I stayed where I was on the climbing frame. I hoped my little family would escape quietly and go for help. But they stood there transfixed. There were three small children, I remember, all under seven. Their mother was with them, and the old man was probably her father. Very sweet, they had been, taking pictures of me holding the smallest child with the two older ones on either side. I didn't want them to come to any harm.

Fortunately the hooligans hardly noticed them. They clubbed the base of the climbing frame with their sticks. They tried to shake me off.

'Hoo-hoo-hoo!' they screamed. 'Come down and we'll give you some nuts.' I didn't move. They could shake that frame all night and it wouldn't budge.

'We'll give it some nuts all right,' they said. 'If it won't get down and fight like a monkey we'll drag it down.'

They swarmed up my frame. They swung on my ropes. I went from level to level to avoid them. If only the family had gone for help – if only the hooligans had been stupid – I might have got away with it.

But it only takes one with a bit of intelligence to organise the other four into a dangerous unit. He was small. He was neat. He had clear blue eyes which blazed with excitement. He was one of those lads who love a challenge. My agility on the climbing frame was a challenge. It became a competition he wanted to win.

He set three of them to drive me to the edge of the frame. The other he put on a rope. As I prepared to haul myself up to the next level he sprung his trap.

'Now!' he screamed.

The lad on the rope swung. I saw him coming but there was nowhere to go. He hit me like an iron pendulum and I flew off the frame and went crashing to the ground. The others dropped on me. I thought my back was broken.

They sorted themselves out soon enough. 'Let's see the bastard,' the leader said. 'Get his fucking mask off.'

They tore King Kong's face off mine and threw it into the bushes.

'Shit!' they said. 'Bloody hell! Look at that.'

The little children, who up till then had only been crying, started to scream.

I can hardly bear to remember what happened next. I

suppose it reminds me too painfully of the past. You see, after the accident, after my face healed, my mother decided that it would be best for me to have plastic surgery to put things right. So I went back into hospital where they broke my cheekbones again and tried to rearrange my eye socket. But something went wrong. It does sometimes. It wasn't anyone's fault. Maybe I rejected my own tissue.

My mother had begun hopefully but after the failure it became harder and harder for the doctors to comfort her. In the end, she took my little sister and went north to Scotland and I never saw her again. It was a relief in a way. Because as she became unable to stand the sight of my face, I became unable to stand the sight of hers. Well, not her face, exactly, more the expression on it. I don't have to look at myself, but I do have to look at the people who are looking at me. I know I am a fright, and when people look at me they become ugly too.

The last line in the movie *King Kong* is: ''Twas beauty killed the beast.' Well, in my experience, it's the other way round. When even the prettiest people look at me they become horrible, so the beast kills beauty.

The little kiddies screamed.

The lad with the clear blue eyes said, 'Shit! No wonder it wears a monkey suit.'

'Come on,' he said, 'Let's get out of here before I throw up.'

I got up. I couldn't find my mask. I took off my gauntlets. I hit him on the side of his handsome head, and when he was down I dropped on his throat with all my weight.

You know, sometimes you find a piece of backbone in a tin of salmon, and when you get it between your teeth it breaks with a soft crunching sound. It was as easy as that.

I shouldn't have done it. I was bigger than him. He was only a kid really – not a child any more but not grown-up either. But at the time it seemed to me he had taken away everything that was mine. All I had was an illusion anyway – the illusion of being a monster. You can't kill someone for that. It just isn't enough.

The funny thing is how nice everyone was about it – even the police. 'I understand,' everyone kept saying. They look at my face and they say, 'I understand,' as if my face tells them everything, as if a disfigured face clearly explains an ugly action. Even the doctors, who are educated men and should know better, think it was years of taunts and rejection which drove me to murder. My solicitor tells me he's sure the court will accept a plea of self-defence. 'They'll understand,' he says confidently.

What if I tell the court I just lost my temper? Suppose I tell them, as I'm telling you, that my face doesn't represent me any more than yours does you? My face is an accident, but I am responsible for my actions. A sad life and an ugly face do not make me any less responsible for losing my temper, do they?

Perhaps they really think I'm King Kong, that I'm not quite human. Just as they feel sorry for King Kong, because although he's a monster he seems to feel human emotions, so they feel sorry for me. If they really thought I was human they'd deal with me the same way they dealt with that man who murdered his girlfriend last month because she threw a plate of baked beans in his face. They don't tell him they understand.

But look on the bright side. Fantasyland has a new regulation now and teenagers are not allowed in unless accompanied by a little child. Apart from that Cherry says it's business as usual. She says it's not the same without me though, and she doesn't think the man who took over my job will last the summer.

'He complains like anything on sunny days,' she told me last time she visited. 'He's got eczema and the itching drives him crazy.'

Cherry should know. Life can be hell for a hot dog too on a sunny day. You don't have to be King Kong to suffer.

DEAR GEORGE

CATHY ACE

Born and raised in south Wales, Cathy Ace graduated from University College Cardiff in 1982. She began to write seriously in 1987, having developed a career in advertising and marketing to the point where she established her own company. Cathy Ace now lives in south London, but visits her family home in Swansea as often as possible.

I

January 1st
So here it is, the first day of the year I kill George. This diary will be a record of all that I do this year, so that one day everyone will know how clever I was. I'll tell you, dear diary, everything. No one else will know our plans – but after ten years of gradually hating dear, sweet George more and more, day after day, month after month, I'm going to do something about it. I'm going to stop him snoring; stop his armpits smelling; stop him scraping his knife on his plate; stop him eyeing up young girls; stop his palms sweating; stop him picking his nose – stop him dead.

I'm going to keep you hidden underneath my one and only frilly nightie. George never looks in the wardrobe drawer where I keep it hidden. So no one will know that you're there except you and me. And we won't be telling, will we?

January 28th
I think I'm doing very well to find the time to tell you all about what's been going on – every day. I find the time because you're very special to me. You understand me – not like him!

He's out at the pub again with his 'mates'! I expect they'll all be sitting there cracking dirty jokes, and he'll be busy chatting up that new barmaid. I saw her in town the other week. Little tart! All boobs and no brain, that's what I say. Mind you, I feel better knowing that I'll be at dear George's funeral in July. Oh, I'm sorry, didn't I tell you? I decided yesterday that I'd kill him on July 4th. It's Independence Day in America you know. Good that, eh? The day I get rid of George will be celebrated right at the other side of the world. Clever.

February 1st

I've been thinking. I don't know how we'll manage when George is dead. I haven't got any money, and I've never had a job. I don't think I could do anything. Except horrible things like working in a shop, or a factory, and I really don't want to do that. I don't know how to get round this one at all. George hasn't got any money. Our savings in the Post Office wouldn't go very far. What shall I do? Oh, yes, that's a good idea. Get George to insure his life, then I get the money when he's dead. You're very clever, aren't you? Almost as clever as me!

February 4th

I'm going to talk to George about life insurance tonight. When he comes to bed I'm going to talk to him about it — all casual like. We agreed £100,000 didn't we? Yes, I know you think that's greedy, but I'll want to live it up a bit when boring old George has gone. I'll tell you tomorrow how it goes. I've got to have a bath now. It's Wednesday; we always do it on a Wednesday, unless George doesn't feel like it. Knowing my luck he will tonight.

February 5th

I had to tell George that I wanted us both to insure ourselves, so as not to make him suspicious, but he says we can't afford it anyway.

I don't believe him. I'm going to get the man from the Pru to come and talk to us; he goes to Iris and David's every month to get his money. Iris is going to ask him to call here next time. Iris said I look tired today. That's because George came in late last night and woke me up. He never smells of drink, but I know he's been drinking. He says he's at the Country and Western Club, but that's just an excuse to go out boozing where he knows I won't follow. Maybe next Wednesday I'll go along with him, see what he really gets up to. That would finish him! That would blow his little cover story for late nights out!

February 12th
Sorry I didn't talk to you last night: I got all dressed up, and when George came in from the office I told him I was going out with him. That shocked him! And you'll never guess what we did – we DID go to the blessed Country and Western Club! Lots of people said hello to him as we went in, lots of women, that is. But he didn't drink at all – only orange juice. He did that to make me think that he never ever drinks, but I know different. Anyway, even though he didn't drink, we still did it when we came home. Honestly, you sit in a corner not talking to anyone, have to listen to that awful racket all night, and still have to come home and do it – terrible! I don't think I'll bother again!

February 27th
We both signed the insurance papers today! The fool! He didn't have a clue! Now when I kill him I'll be rich too! I can hardly wait. The 4th July seems a very long time away. Perhaps I should reconsider that date. As soon as he's out of the way I can go on a lovely cruise: people would expect me to get away for a while after all the fuss and police and all that. I suppose there will be a fuss. What do you think? Yes, I think so too. But it's the only way to do it – shoot George then give myself up to the police and tell them it was An Accident. Besides, I want to see his face as I pull the trigger – see his stupid eyes show the realisation of what I'm doing to him: see him getting the point for once in his stupid, miserable life.

It's all his fault anyway, for keeping the gun. If I hadn't seen it in his desk last year I'd never have got this brilliant idea. It's probably illegal to have the gun here: but *that's* all right with dear George because it was his high and mighty father's! I'm going to take it onto the Common next week to check that it works; there are only three bullets in it but I need to use one just to make sure I know how to make it shoot properly. I'll

take the car on Saturday and wait until there's no one around –
so long as I don't point it at anything except the ground it can't
do any harm. Anyway, goodnight now. I'm sorry I haven't
been writing in you as tidily as usual today, but that copperplate is very hard to keep going, and my hands are sore from
wringing out the bedroom curtains this afternoon. Still, the
washing-machine man will be here tomorrow and then the
spinner will be working again.

March 7th

I shot the gun today! I didn't realise it would make such a
noise! It frightened me to death! (What a funny thing to say – it
won't frighten George to death, it'll shoot George to death!)
No one heard me though; it was far too cold for anyone to be
out on the Common. I hurt my wrist, too; I held the gun in two
hands like they do on the telly, but it still pushed back a lot. At
least I know I can do it.

And dear George didn't suspect anything, of course. I asked
if I could borrow the car to go to Legge's, over near Madge's
and I put the gun in the bottom of my blue shopping bag
wrapped in an old carrier bag. He just sat there glued to the
bloody football and threw the keys at me. I nearly laughed – if
only he'd guessed! Him and his beloved West Ham – well, it's
the last season I'll have to put up with *Match of the Day*. Come
to think of it, I wouldn't mind shooting Jimmy Hill too!

March 12th

Did the washing today. One thing I really hate is the way
George refuses to use Kleenex, and will insist on using real
hankies. I'm the one who's got to wash them! They're revolting! But he won't listen to me. I'd make him wash them
himself, but he wouldn't get them clean, and I'm certainly not
having her next door seeing dirty washing on the line. I was
doing the ironing when I tried to work out how many of
George's shirts I've ironed since we've been married – it's
about 4,000. Probably more. I feel as though I've done them all
today! I'm getting tired more quickly these days. Getting
headaches too. George isn't at all sympathetic. He says I
should get my eyes seen to. He'll find out if there's anything
wrong with my eyes when I hit him with that little bullet!

April 27th

Our Wedding Anniversary! What a bundle of laughs today was, dear diary. I gave George a card and a new pair of grey woollen socks from Marks and Spencers. He gave me a box of chocolates – then he ate all the soft ones! Pig! I hate him! Do you know he actually laughed at me as he ate the coffee cream! That was IT. Dear, dear diary, I know we agreed that we'd wait, but I *can't* wait any longer. He's a pig. He hates me as much as I hate him, I'm sure of that, he wouldn't have eaten all the soft ones if he didn't would he?

Eleven years ago today I promised to love, honour and obey him. Well today I'm promising to love, honour and obey myself. Please don't be upset, I'll keep you in the picture. I'm going to do it this Saturday. Then there'll just be you and me, and the money too, of course!

May 2nd

I know I'm early, but I had to talk to you – I'm so excited! I've smashed the glass in the back door, inwards like we agreed, and I've put my big shopping bag in the middle of the living room and filled it with all our bits of silver. It's already dark, but the gun is safe in my dressing-gown pocket. I'll tell the police I was in bed with a headache when I heard the noise, picked up the gun and went downstairs. I'll tell them how terrified I was, and when I saw a shadowy figure at the door coming towards me, that I thought it was a burglar, or a rapist, and shot at it. Then I'll tell them how I discovered it was dear George. They'll see how upset I am and I'll get away with it! Then it will be just the three of us. You, me and the money. It won't be long now. He never puts the light on when he comes in. I'll put you away now. We may not be able to talk for some time.

II

The foreman of the jury rose from his seat.

'Not guilty.'

Clear and loud NOT GUILTY! It was An Accident – a dreadful, tragic Accident. The past few days had been a tremendous strain: the newspapers had picked up the story, and photographs of 'The Victim' and 'The Accused' had appeared everywhere. But now it was over, the jury agreed with the general public – tragic, but certainly not premeditated. The judge was saying something, then there were lots of congratulations being shouted from the gallery. Outside were more photographers, and, thankfully, a taxi. Not back to the house – not that porch where it had happened. No, to a hotel room: a bright, impersonal room with just a hint of luxury. Oh yes, that insurance money would come in very handy!

III

George Melrose turned on the television set, then bounced on the edge of the hotel bed. The afternoon film crackled in monochrome – there was Katherine Hepburn in a dressing gown, just like Joyce when she had come downstairs that night. George had looked at her disapproving eyes peering from underneath her curlers for the last time, walked towards her, took her hands, pointed the gun towards her heart and pulled the trigger. The blood had ruined the dressing gown of course. Then he had put the gun in Joyce's hand and shot again, this time breaking the glass in the big oak hallstand.

The police hadn't believed George that Joyce had been trying to kill him. He had never thought they would. After all, George was such an inoffensive chap, why should Joyce want to kill him? Unless she had a screw loose, of course. No, George was quiet, a tea-totaller who was hard-working, and happy to stay at home watching the box. No one had known him to go out except to his Country and Western Club, where he was a respected and diligent Club Secretary – they'd all come to the court to say so!

The police hadn't known what to believe, until they found the diary. It really had been very clever of him to hide it under her nightie: for months it had been hidden in the glove compartment of the car, in a plastic bag to keep it clean. George had carefully filled in each day's entry in painstakingly formed copperplate, just as in the calligraphy book now also to be found in Joyce's wardrobe.

31

George rang room service and ordered a cream tea. The weather was brightening, perhaps the blossom would liven itself up a bit now, thought George. Joyce had liked the blossom: it made her sneeze though, of course! Miserable, boring, plain, stupid Joyce. It really was incredible that everyone now believed she could have been bright enough to think up what was, after all, a very clever plan! People were so stupid!

IV

Inspector Glover and his wife were having a late supper. They rarely discussed work, but the Melrose case had aroused much interest nationwide, and Glover's name had become known as a result. Betty Glover collected the dirty plates from the table and pushed them into the soapy water in the sink.

'You look tired, Evan.'

'It's been a hard day. I won't be sorry to get off to bed.'

'Look, Evan, I know we don't usually talk about things, but if you want to chat about this one – you go ahead.'

Evan Glover finished his tea and carefully placed the cup in the centre of the recess in the saucer.

'Don't worry, love, a good night's sleep will cure me. I just haven't felt right about this Melrose case all along – there's something we've missed, but not something you can put your finger on. And no matter how much of a gut feeling I've got, you can't convict a man on the basis of my indigestion. Anyway, he's cleared. That diary did it – all the experts agreed it was the work of someone with a few marbles loose. Almost childlike. Still, it made it perfectly clear she intended to do him in. Even covered the double insurance angle. Nice chap, you know. Quiet, almost invisible, quite colourless. Yes, that's it, colourless.'

Betty Glover wiped her hands on the tea towel, then spread the dishcloth over the taps to dry.

'Put some water in that cup before you come up, Evan. I'm going to make a move now. Don't you be too long.'

'Night, love,' called Evan to the receding figure.

'Mind you,' called back his wife, 'if I was going to kill you and give myself up straight away I'd never put my hair in curlers. Everyone looks awful in curlers. She must have been mad!'

Evan Glover was stunned. He stared open-mouthed at the china cabinet as though it had uttered the words itself . . .

HAVE A NICE DEATH

ANTONIA FRASER

Lady Antonia is the eldest of the Earl and Countess of
Longford's eight children. Both Lord Longford and the Coun-
tess of Longford have had work published. The Countess of
Longford is at present writing her autobiography.

Lady Antonia is a graduate of Oxford University where she
obtained an Honours Degree in History.

She is the author of three historical biographies: *Mary
Queen of Scots* (1969) which won the James Tait Black
Prize and was an international bestseller, being translated
into eight languages; *Cromwell, our Chief of Men* (1973),
and *King Charles II* (1979), both bestsellers in Britain and
the United States. She has also written *King James VI* in the
Kings and Queens of England series, of which she was the
General Editor. Her mysteries featuring Jemima Shore,
Investigator, have been the subject of a twelve-part television series. She has contributed articles to many magazines, including 'History Today' and literary reviews. She
has broadcast on numerous occasions on both radio and
television, including 'Call My Bluff' and she won the
'Going for a Song' TV broadcast on three consecutive
occasions.

She is married to playwright Harold Pinter; they live in
London.

Have a Nice Death appeared in *John Creasey's Crime Collection*,
1984

Everyone was being extraordinarily courteous to Sammy Luke
in New York.

34

Take Sammy's arrival at Kennedy Airport, for example: Sammy had been quite struck by the warmth of the welcome. Sammy thought: how relieved Zara would be! Zara (his wife) was inclined to worry about Sammy – he had to admit, with some cause; in the past, that is. In the past Sammy had been nervous, delicate, highly strung, whatever you liked to call it – Sammy suspected that some of Zara's women friends had a harsher name for it; the fact was that things tended to go wrong where Sammy was concerned, unless Zara was there to iron them out. But that was in England. Sammy was quite sure he was not going to be nervous in America; perhaps, cured by the New World, he would never be nervous again.

Take the immigration officials – hadn't Sammy been warned about them?

'They're nothing but gorillas' – Zara's friend, wealthy Tess, who travelled frequently to the States, had pronounced the word in a dark voice. For an instant Sammy, still in his nervous English state, visualised immigration checkpoints manned by terrorists armed with machine guns. But the official seated in a booth, who summoned Sammy in, was slightly built, perhaps even slighter than Sammy himself though the protection of the booth made it difficult to tell. And he was smiling as he cried:

'C'mon, c'mon, bring the family!' A notice outside the booth stated that only one person – or one family – was permitted inside at a time.

'I'm afraid my wife's not travelling with me,' stated Sammy apologetically.

'I sure wish my wife wasn't with me either,' answered the official, with ever-increasing bonhomie.

Sammy wondered confusedly – it had been a long flight after all – whether he should explain his own very different feelings about his wife, his passionate regret that Zara had not been able to accompany him. But his new friend was already examining his passport, flipping through a large black directory, talking again:

'A writer . . . . Would I know any of your books?'

This was an opportunity for Sammy to explain intelligently the purpose of his visit. Sammy Luke was the author of six novels. Five of them had sold well, if not astoundingly well, in England and not at all in the United States. The sixth, *Women*

Weeping, due perhaps to its macabrely fashionable subject-matter, had hit some kind of publishing jackpot in both countries. Only a few weeks after publication in the States, its sales were phenomenal and rising; an option on the film rights (maybe Jane Fonda and Meryl Streep as the masochists?) had already been bought. As a result of all this, Sammy's new American publishers believed hotly that only one further thing was necessary to ensure the vast, the *total* success of *Women Weeping* in the States, and that was to make of its author a television celebrity. Earnestly defending his own position on the subject of violence and female masochism in a series of television interviews and talk shows, Sammy Luke was expected to shoot *Women Weeping* high, high into the best-seller lists and keep it there. All this was the firm conviction of Sammy's editor at Porlock Publishers, Clodagh Jansen.

'You'll be great on the talk shows, Sammy,' Clodagh had cawed down the line from the States. 'So little and cute and then – ' Clodagh made a loud noise with her lips as if someone was gobbling someone else up. Presumably it was not Sammy who was to be gobbled. Clodagh was a committed feminist, as she had carefully explained to Sammy on her visit to England, when she had bought *Women Weeping*, against much competition, for a huge sum. But she believed in the social role of best-sellers like *Women Weeping* to finance radical feminist works. Sammy had tried to explain that his book was in no way anti-feminist, no way at all, witness the fact that Zara herself, his Egeria, had not complained –

'Save it for the talk shows, Sammy,' was all that Clodagh had replied.

While Sammy was still wondering how to put all this concisely, but to his best advantage, at Kennedy Airport, the man in the booth asked: 'And the purpose of your visit, Mr Luke?'

Sammy was suddenly aware that he had drunk a great deal on the long flight – courtesy of Porlock's First Class ticket – and slept too heavily as well. His head began to sing. But whatever answer he gave, it was apparently satisfactory. The man stamped the white sheet inside his passport and handed it back. Then:

'Enjoy your visit to the United States of America, Mr Luke. Have a nice day now.'

'Oh I will, I know I will,' promised Sammy. 'It seems a lovely day here already.'

Sammy's experiences at the famous Barraclough Hotel (accommodation arranged by Clodagh) were if anything even more heart-warming. Everyone, but everyone at the Barraclough wanted Sammy to enjoy himself during his visit.

'Have a nice day now, Mr Luke': most conversations ended like that, whether they were with the hotel telephonists, the agreeable men who operated the lifts or the gentlemanly *concierge*. Even the New York taxi drivers, from whose guarded expressions Sammy would not otherwise have suspected such warm hearts, wanted Sammy to have a nice day.

'Oh I will, I will,' Sammy began by answering. After a bit he added: 'I just adore New York,' said with a grin and the very suspicion of an American twang.

'This is the friendliest city in the world,' he told Zara down the long-distance telephone, shouting, so that his words were accompanied by little vibratory echoes.

'Tess says they don't really mean it.' Zara's voice in contrast was thin, diminished into a tiny wail by the line. 'They're not sincere, you know.'

'Tess was wrong about the gorillas at Immigration. She could be wrong about that too. Tess doesn't *own* the whole country you know. She just inherited a small slice of it.'

'Darling, you do sound funny,' countered Zara; her familiar anxiety on the subject of Sammy made her sound stronger. 'Are you all right? I mean, are you all right over there all by yourself – '

'I'm mainly on television during the day,' Sammy cut in with a laugh. 'Alone except for the chat show host and forty million people.' Sammy was deciding whether to add, truthfully, that actually not all the shows were networked; some of his audiences being as low as a million, or say a million and a half, when he realised that Zara was saying in a voice of distinct reproach:

'And you haven't asked after Mummy yet.' It was the sudden illness of Zara's mother, another person emotionally dependent upon her, which had prevented Zara's trip to New York with Sammy, at the last moment.

It was only after Sammy had rung off – having asked

tenderly after Zara's mother and apologised for his crude crack about Tess before doing so – that he realised Zara was quite right. He *had* sounded rather funny: even to himself. That is, he would never have dared to make such a remark about Tess in London. Dared? Sammy pulled himself up.

To Zara, his strong and lovely Zara, he could of course say anything. She was his wife. As a couple, they were exceptionally close as all their circle agreed; being childless (a decision begun through poverty in the early days and somehow never rescinded) only increased their intimacy. Because their marriage had not been founded on a flash-in-the-pan sexual attraction but something deeper, more companionate – sex had never played a great part in it, even at the beginning – the bond had only grown stronger with the years. Sammy doubted whether there was a more genuinely united pair in London.

All this was true; and comforting to recollect. It was just that in recent years Tess had become an omnipresent force in their lives: Tess on clothes, Tess on interior decoration, especially Tess on curtains, that was the real pits – a new expression which Sammy had picked up from Clodagh; and somehow Tess's famous money always seemed to reinforce her opinions in a way which was rather curious, considering Zara's own radical contempt for unearned wealth.

'Well I've got money now. Lots and lots of it. Earned money,' thought Sammy, squaring his thin shoulders in the new pale blue jacket which Zara, yes Zara, had made him buy. He looked in one of the huge gilded mirrors which decorated his suite at the Barraclough, pushing aside the large floral arrangement, a gift from the hotel manager (or was it Clodagh?) to do so. Sammy Luke, the conqueror of New York or at least American television; then he had to laugh at his own absurdity.

He went on to the little balcony which let off the suite's sitting-room and looked down at the ribbon of streets which stretched below; the roofs of lesser buildings; the blur of green where Central Park nestled, at his disposal, in the centre of it all. The plain truth was that he was just very very happy. The reason was not purely the success of his book, nor even his instant highly commercial fame, as predicted by Clodagh, on television, nor yet the attentions of the Press, parts of which had after all been quite violently critical of his book, again as predicted by Clodagh. The reason was that Sammy Luke felt loved in New York in a vast, wonderful, impersonal way. Nothing was demanded of him by this love; it was like an electric fire which simulated red-hot coals even when it was switched off. New York glowed but it could not scorch. In his heart Sammy knew that he had never been so happy before.

It was at this point that the telephone rang again. Sammy left the balcony. Sammy was expecting one of three calls. The first, and most likely, was Clodagh's daily checking call: 'Hi, Sammy, it's Clodagh Pegoda . . . listen, that show was great, the one they taped. Our publicity girl actually told me it didn't go too well at the time, she was frightened they were mauling you . . . but the way it come out . . . Zouch!' More interesting sounds from Clodagh's mobile and rather sensual lips. 'That's my Sam. You really had them licked. I guess the little girl was just protective. Sue-May, was it? Joanie. Yes, Joanie. She's crazy about you. I'll have to talk to her; what's a nice girl like that doing being crazy about a man, and a married man at that . . . .'

Clodagh's physical preference for her own sex was a robust joke between them; it was odd how being in New York made that too innocuous. In England Sammy had been secretly rather shocked by the frankness of Clodagh's allusions: more alarmingly she had once goosed him, apparently fooling, but with the accompanying words, 'You're a bit like a girl your-self, Sammy,' which were not totally reassuring. Even that was preferable to the embarrassing occasion when Clodagh had playfully declared a physical attraction to Zara, wondered – outside the money that was now coming in – how Zara put up with Sammy. In New York, however, Sammy entered enthu-siastically into the fun.

He was also pleased to hear, however lightly meant, that Joanie, the publicity girl in charge of his day-to-day arrange-ments, was crazy about him; for Joanie, unlike handsome, piratical, frightening Clodagh, was small and tender.

The second possibility for the call was Joanie herself. In which case she would be down in the lobby of the Barraclough, ready to escort him to an afternoon taping at a television studio across town. Later Joanie would drop Sammy back at the Barraclough, paying carefully and slightly earnestly for the taxi as though Sammy's nerves might be ruffled if the ceremony was not carried out correctly. One of these days, Sammy thought with a smile, he might even ask Joanie up to his suite at the Barraclough . . . after all what were suites for? (Sammy had never had a suite in a hotel before, his English publisher having an old-fashioned taste for providing his authors with plain bedrooms while on promotional tours.)

The third possibility was that Zara was calling him back: their conversation, for all Sammy's apologies, had not really ended on a satisfactory note; alone in London, Zara was doubtless feeling anxious about Sammy as a result. He detected a little complacency in himself about Zara: after all, there was for once nothing for her to feel anxious about (except perhaps Joanie, he added to himself with a smile).

Sammy's complacency was shattered by the voice on the telephone:

'I saw you on television last night,' began the voice – female, whispering. 'You bastard, Sammy Luke, I'm coming up to your room and I'm going to cut off your little – ' A detailed anatomical description followed of what the voice was going to do to Sammy Luke. The low violent obscenities, so horrible, so surprising, coming out of the innocent white hotel telephone, continued for a while unstopped, assaulting his ears like the rustle of some appalling cowrie shell; until Sammy thought to clutch the instrument to his chest, and thus stifle the voice in the surface of his new blue jacket.

After a moment, thinking he might have put an end to the terrible whispering, Sammy raised the instrument again. He was in time to hear the voice say:

'Have a nice death, Mr Luke.'

Then there was silence.

Sammy felt quite sick. A moment later he was running across the ornate sitting room of the splendid Barraclough suite, retching; the bathroom seemed miles away at the far end of the spacious bedroom; he only just reached it in time.

Sammy was lying, panting, on the nearest twin bed to the door – the one which had been meant for Zara – when the telephone rang again. He picked it up and held it at a distance, then recognised the merry interested voice of the hotel telephonist.

'Oh, Mr Luke,' she was saying, 'while your line was busy just now Joanie Lazlo called from Porlock Publishers, and she'll call right back. But she says to tell you that the taping for this afternoon has been cancelled, Max Syegrand is still tied up on the Coast and can't make it. Too bad about that, Mr Luke. It's a good show. Anyway, she'll come by this evening with some more books to sign . . . Have a nice day now, Mr Luke,' and the merry telephonist rang off. But this time Sammy shuddered when he heard the familiar cheerful farewell.

It seemed a long time before Joanie rang to say that she was downstairs in the hotel lobby, and should she bring the copies of *Women Weeping* up to the suite? When she arrived at the sitting-room door, carrying a Mexican tote bag weighed down by books, Joanie's pretty little pink face was glowing and she gave Sammy her usual softly enthusiastic welcome. All the same Sammy could hardly believe that he had contemplated seducing her – or indeed anyone – in his gilded suite amid the floral arrangements. That all seemed a very long while ago.

For in the hours before Joanie's arrival, Sammy received two more calls. The whispering voice grew bolder still in its descriptions of Sammy's fate; but it did not grow stronger. For some reason, Sammy listened through the first call to the end. At last the phrase came: although he was half expecting it, his heart still thumped when he heard the words:

'Have a nice death now, Mr Luke.'

With the second call, he slammed down the telephone immediately and then called back the operator:

'No more,' he said loudly and rather breathlessly, 'No more, I don't want any more.'

'Pardon me, Mr Luke?'

'I meant, I don't want any more calls, not like that, not now.'

'All righty.' The operator – it was another voice, not the merry woman who habitually watched television, but just as friendly. 'I'll hold your calls for now, Mr Luke. I'll be happy to do it. Goodbye now. Have a nice evening.'

Should Sammy have questioned this new operator about his recent caller? No doubt she would declare herself happy to discuss the matter. But he dreaded a further cheerful impersonal New York encounter in his shaken state. Beside, the very first call had been put through by the merry television-watcher. Zara. He needed to talk to Zara. She would know what to do; or rather she would know what *he* should do.

'What's going on?' she exclaimed. 'I tried to ring you three times and that bloody woman on the hotel switchboard wouldn't put me through. Are you all right? I rang you back because you sounded so peculiar. Sort of high, you were laughing at things, things which weren't really funny, its not like you, is it, in New York people are supposed to get this energy, but I never thought – '

'I'm not all right, not all right at all,' Sammy interrupted her; he was aware of a high, rather tremulous note in his voice. 'I was all right then, more than all right, but now I'm not, not at all.' Zara couldn't at first grasp what Sammy was telling her, and in the end he had to abandon all explanations of his previous state of exhilaration. For one thing Zara couldn't seem to grasp what he was saying, and for another Sammy was guiltily aware that absence from Zara's side had played more than a little part in this temporary madness. So Sammy settled for agreeing that he had been acting rather oddly since he had arrived in New York, and then appealed to Zara to advise him how next to proceed.

Once Sammy had made this admission, Zara sounded more like her normal brisk but caring self. She told Sammy to ring up Clodagh at Porlock.

'Frankly, Sammy, I can't think why you didn't ring her straight away.' Zara pointed out that if Sammy could not, Clodagh certainly could and would deal with the hotel switchboard, so that calls were filtered, the lawful distinguished from the unlawful.

'Clodagh might even know the woman,' observed Sammy weakly at one point. 'She has some very odd friends.'

Zara laughed. 'Not *that* odd, I hope.' Altogether she was in a better temper. Sammy remembered to ask after Zara's mother before he rang off; and on hearing that Tess had flown to America on business, he went so far as to say that he would love to have a drink with her.

When Joanie arrived in the suite, Sammy told her about the threatening calls and was vaguely gratified by her distress.

'I think that's just dreadful, Sammy,' she murmured, her light hazel eyes swimming with some tender emotion. 'Clodagh's not in the office right now, but let me talk with the hotel manager right away . . . .' Yet it was odd how Joanie no longer seemed in the slightest bit attractive to Sammy. There was even something cloying about her friendliness; perhaps there was a shallowness there, a surface brightness concealing nothing; perhaps Tess was right and New Yorkers were after all insincere. All in all, Sammy was pleased to see Joanie depart with the signed books.

He did not offer her a second drink, although she had brought him an advance copy of the *New York Times* book section for Sunday, showing that *Women Weeping* had jumped four places in the best-seller list.

'Have a nice evening, Sammy,' said Joanie softly as she closed the door of the suite. 'I've left a message with Clodagh's answering service and I'll call you tomorrow.'

But Sammy did not have a very nice evening. Foolishly he decided to have dinner in his suite; the reason was that he had some idiotic lurking fear that the woman with the whispering voice would be lying in wait for him outside the Barraclough.

'Have a nice day,' said the waiter automatically who delivered the meal on a heated trolley covered in a white damask cloth, after Sammy had signed the chit. Sammy hated him.

'The day is over. It is evening.' Sammy spoke in a voice which was pointed, almost vicious; he had just deposited a tip on the white chit. By this time the waiter, stowing the dollars rapidly and expertly in his pocket was already on his way to the door; he turned and flashed a quick smile:

'Yeah. Sure. Thank you, Mr Luke. Have a nice day.' The waiter's hand was on the door handle.

'It is evening here!' exclaimed Sammy. He found he was shaking. 'Do you understand? Do you agree that it is *evening*?' The man, mildly startled, but not at all discomposed, said again: 'Yeah. Sure. Evening. Goodbye now.' And he went.

Sammy poured himself a whisky from the suite's mini-bar. He no longer felt hungry. The vast white expanse of his dinner trolley depressed him, because it reminded him of his encounter with the waiter; at the same time he lacked the courage to push the trolley boldly out of the suite into the corridor. Having avoided leaving the Barraclough he now found that even more foolishly he did not care to open the door of his own suite.

Clodagh being out of the office, it was doubtless Joanie's fault that the hotel operators still ignored their instructions. Another whispering call was let through, about ten o'clock at night, as Sammy was watching a movie starring the young Elizabeth Taylor, much cut up by commercials, on television. (If he stayed awake till midnight, he could see himself on one of the talk shows he had recorded.) The operator was now supposed to announce the name of each caller, for Sammy's inspection; but this call came straight through.

There was a nasty new urgency in what the voice was promising: 'Have a nice death now. I'll be coming by quite soon, Sammy Luke.'

In spite of the whisky − he drained yet another of the tiny bottles − Sammy was still shaking when he called down to the operator and protested: 'I'm still getting these calls. You've got to do something. You're supposed to be keeping them away from me.'

The operator, not a voice he recognised, sounded rather puzzled, but full of goodwill; spurious goodwill, Sammy now felt. Even if she was sincere, she was certainly stupid. She did not seem to recall having put through anyone to Sammy within the last ten minutes. Sammy did not dare instruct her to hold all calls in case Zara rang up again (or Clodagh, for that matter; where was Clodagh, now that he needed protection from this kind of feminist nut?) He felt too desperate to cut himself off altogether from contact with the outside world. What would Zara advise?

The answer was really quite simple, once it had occurred to him. Sammy rang down to the front desk and complained to the house manager who was on night duty. The house manager, like the operator, was rather puzzled, but extremely polite.

'Threats, Mr Luke? I assure you you'll be very secure at the Barraclough. We have guards naturally, and we are accustomed . . . but if you'd like me to come up to discuss the matter, why I'd be happy to . . . .'

When the house manager arrived, he was quite charming. He referred not only to Sammy's appearance on television but to his actual book. He told Sammy he'd loved the book; what was more he'd given another copy to his eighty-three-year-old mother (who'd seen Sammy on the *Today* show) and she'd loved it too. Sammy was too weary to wonder more than passingly what an eighty-three-year-old mother would make of *Women Weeping*. He was further depressed by the house manager's elaborate courtesy; it wasn't absolutely clear whether he believed Sammy's story, or merely thought he was suffering from the delightful strain of being a celebrity. Maybe the guests at the Barraclough behaved like that all the time, describing imaginary death threats? That possibility also Sammy was too exhausted to explore.

At midnight he turned the television on again and watched himself, on the chat show in the blue jacket, laughing and wriggling with his own humour, denying for the tenth time that he had any curious sadistic tastes himself, that *Women Weeping* was founded on any incident in his private life.

When the telephone rang sharply into the silence of the suite shortly after the end of the show, Sammy knew that it would be his persecutor; nevertheless the sight of his erstwhile New York self, so debonair, so confident, had given him back some strength. Sammy was no longer shaking as he picked up the receiver.

It was Clodagh on the other end of the line, who had just returned to New York from somewhere out of town and picked up Joanie's message from her answering service. Clodagh listened carefully to what Sammy had to say and answered him with something less than her usual loud-hailing zest.

'I'm not too happy about this one!' she said after what – for Clodagh – was quite a lengthy silence. 'Ever since Andy Warhol, we can never be quite sure what these jokers will do. Maybe a press release tomorrow? Sort of protect you with publicity *and* sell a few more copies. Maybe not. I'll think about that one, I'll call Joanie in the morning.' To Sammy's relief, Clodagh was in charge.

There was another pause. When Clodagh spoke again, her tone was kindly, almost maternal; she reminded him, surprisingly, of Zara.

'Listen, little Sammy, stay right there and I'll be over. We don't want to lose an author, do we?'

Sammy went on to the little balcony which led off the sitting-room and gazed down at the street lights far far below; he did not gaze too long, partly because Sammy suffered from vertigo (although that had become much better in New York) and partly because he wondered whether an enemy was waiting for him down below. Sammy no longer thought all the lights were twinkling with goodwill. Looking downward he imagined Clodagh, a strong Zara-substitute, striding towards him to save him.

When Clodagh did arrive, rather suddenly at the door of the suite – maybe she did not want to alarm him by telephoning up from the lobby of the hotel? – she did look very strong, as well as handsome, in her black designer jeans and black silk shirt; through her shirt he could see the shape of her flat muscular chest, with the nipples clearly defined, like the chest of a young Greek athlete.

'Little Sammy,' said Clodagh quite tenderly. 'Who would want to frighten you?'

The balcony windows were still open. Clodagh made Sammy pour himself yet another whisky and one for her too (there was a trace of the old Clodagh in the acerbity with which she gave these orders). Masterfully she also imposed two mysterious bomb-like pills upon Sammy which she promised, together with the whisky, would give him sweet dreams 'and no nasty calls to frighten you'.

Because Clodagh was showing a tendency to stand very close to him, one of her long arms affectionately and irre-moveably round his shoulders, Sammy was not all that unhappy when Clodagh ordered him to take both their drinks on to the balcony, away from the slightly worrying intimacy of the suite.

Sammy stood at the edge of the parapet, holding both glasses, and looked downwards. He felt better. Some of his previous benevolence towards New York came flooding back as the whisky and pills began to take effect. Sammy no longer imagined that his enemy was down there in the street outside the Barraclough, waiting for him.

In a way of course, Sammy was quite right. For Sammy's enemy was not down there in the street below, but standing silently right there behind him, on the balcony, black gloves on her big capable strong hands where they extended from the cuffs of her chic black silk shirt.

'Have a nice death now, Sammy Luke.' Even the familiar phrase hardly had time to strike a chill in his heart as Sammy found himself falling, falling into the deep trough of the New York street twenty-three stories below. The two whisky glasses flew from his hands and little icy glass fragments scattered far and wide, far far from Sammy's tiny slumped body where it hit the pavement; the whisky vanished altogether, for no one recorded drops of whisky falling on their face in Madison Avenue.

Soft-hearted Joanie cried when the police showed her Sammy's typewritten suicide note with that signature so familiar from the signing of the books; the text itself the last product of the battered portable typewriter Sammy had brought with him to New York. But Joanie had to confirm Sammy's distressed state at her last visit to the suite; an impression more than confirmed by the amount of whisky Sammy had consumed before his death – a glass in each hand as he fell, said the police – to say nothing of the pills.

The waiter contributed to the picture too.

'I guess the guy seemed quite upset when I brought him his dinner.' He added as an afterthought: 'He was pretty lonesome too. Wanted to talk. You know the sort. Tried to stop me going away. Wanted to have a conversation. I shoulda stopped but I was busy.' The waiter was genuinely regretful.

The hotel manager was regretful too, which considering the fact that Sammy's death had been duly reported in the Press as occurring from a Barraclough balcony, was decent of him.

One of the operators – Sammy's merry friend – went further and was dreadfully distressed: 'Jesus, I don't believe it. For Christ's sake, I just saw him on television!' The other operator made a calmer statement, simply saying that Sammy had seemed very indecisive about whether he wished to receive calls or not in the course of the evening.

Zara Luke, in England, told the story of Sammy's last day and his pathetic tales of persecution, not otherwise substantiated. She also revealed – not totally to the surprise of her friends – that Sammy had a secret history of mental breakdown and was particularly scared of travelling by himself.

'I shall always blame myself for letting him go,' ended Zara, brokenly.

Clodagh Jansen of Porlock Publishers made a dignified statement about the tragedy.

It was Clodagh too who met the author's widow at the airport when Zara flew out a week later to make all the dreadful arrangements consequent upon poor Sammy's death.

At the airport Clodagh and Zara embraced discreetly, tearfully. It was only in private later at Clodagh's apartment – for Zara to stay at the Barraclough would certainly have been totally inappropriate – that more intimate caresses of a richer quality began. Began, but did not end: neither had any reason to hurry things.

'After all, we've all the time in the world' murmured Sammy's widow to Sammy's publisher.

'And all the money too' Clodagh whispered back; she must remember to tell Zara that *Women Weeping* would reach the Number One spot in the bestseller list on Sunday.

CHASING THE DRAGON

SARAH BARTLETT

Sarah Bartlett started her career as International Press Officer for EMI Records and left to become Studio Manager at a major West End recording studio. After having her first short story published she decided to commit herself to writing fiction full-time. She is now working on her second crime novel based on characters created in *Chasing the Dragon* and has also completed a black comedy script for TV. She is 35, married and has two children.

The first thing Bella Reeves did when she came home and found her husband Carlo naked and dead on the Persian rug was call the police. The second thing she did was phone me.

I was expecting her usual cool arrogance; the only thing that ever moved Bella Reeves was her own talent; yet she was heated, almost breathless as she spoke quickly at the other end of the phone.

'I've called the police, Gaby, Jesus, I think he must have OD'd, I can smell smack a mile off, but there's something else . . .'

It was four-thirty, the central London summer traffic would already be jamming outside my newspaper's office. I was in the City, Bella lived in Chelsea.

'I'll be there as soon as I can. Give me forty-five minutes.'

So Carlo Reeves had died of a probable overdose, had been on the dope for too long and had got away with living, until today. Hell, he'd been an idiot at college, mad enough to marry Bella and dumb enough to get involved with Ralph Stone, a fortune hunter who promised him power and wealth and a dazzling career. They'd run a seedy antiques business, exporting junk to the States. But Carlo had spent most of the time suffering acute bouts of depression and visits to cold-turkey clinics.

Ralph was indecently smart; I'd never liked him. He was too clever, too unwilling to look you in the eye and smile. He was always unshaven, yet somehow, at some time of day he must have dragged a razor across that permanently tanned face. He had always resented Carlo for grabbing Bella at college and used them both, subtly, slowly, greedily, a feeding dingo waiting for the bones. Carlo used to say, 'You'll be a bloody success as a journalist Gaby – stick at it babe, don't go Bella's way, afraid of challenge, hiding in warehouses in Deptford and pretending to paint reality. Hell, what does she know of *life*?'

Sometimes Carlo made me laugh. I had cared a lot for his friendship, his support, but he should have known better, should have listened to his own sermons for once. His death wasn't totally unexpected, fifteen years of coke, maybe three of heroin, both had aged him, soured his energy and youth. Yet recently when we'd bumped glasses in bars in Soho or at Bella's dipso 'showings' he seemed fresh again, alive, beyond the gutter, as if someone other than Bella had pulled a cracker in his pants.

I found an out-of-order parking meter and wondered how soon Ralph Stone would pitch up at Bella's door. A few years ago he had married a brilliant dentist called Deanna. No doubt she'd lose the bastard to Bella's bed, but I couldn't believe she'd really care. I remembered a New Year dinner party at which she'd cried because the sardines still had their eyes attached and laughed when Ralph Stone nibbled Bella's ear.

Drug Squad and Kale Lambert were just getting out of the lift at the bottom of Bella's mansion block when I arrived. I was late, the drive had taken well over an hour and I was in no mood for meeting blasts from the past. Eight years ago Kale had only passion for his work and intolerance for women. He had clumsy hair and wore old fifties shirts and a shabby pair of sneakers. He was a big boy in the Drug Squad now, sometimes we met in unlikely places if I was poking around for a story. For once he looked pleased to see me.

'Hey Gaby, what the hell are you doing here?'

'Bella Reeves is an old mate of mine. I'm not here for the story, Kale, OK?' I pushed past him into the lift.

'Find out who the pusher is, Gaby. I think that woman knows something.'

'It was an overdose then – heroin?'

'Yeah, but looks like suicide, no accident. Listen I'm sorry about . . . .'

'See you Kale.'

In the white, echoing rooms of Bella's empty flat only a chalk line on the Persian rug and the smell of sandalwood soap reminded me that Carlo had once lived there. I poured myself a double vodka and sat down beside Bella.

'Ballet Rambert and his merry band have just gone, they've taken the note. Jesus, I can't believe it, Gaby, it's crazy!'

'What note? What sort of note, Bella?'

'It was lying beside his hand. All wrinkled up like his balls. He must have just got out of the bath.'

'Are you sure?'

'Yeah. There was water still in the tub, sandalwood oil, God how he loved to stink like a woman, for a woman, not me any more, not me!'

'They say it was . . .'

'Suicide? Maybe. The stupid bastard must have halluci-nated in the bath or suddenly remembered to give us all a shock and dropped dead while he was scrawling the wretched thing.'

'What did it say?'

'Just the beginning of a sentence – "I can't get through . . ." – life, another day, to the world, to himself, to me. I don't know.'

I looked down at the white outline of Carlo's death pose and wondered what had wrenched him from the tranquillity of the bath. It was bizarre that he should have bothered to write to anyone.

Bella started to shiver. It was August, hot sweltering London weather. The blinds were still up. I pulled them down and threw Bella my jacket.

'I hope Lambert didn't give you a hard time, Bella. He's all right really, just in love with himself, you know the type.'

'He's that cop that screwed you up a few years back, isn't he? Quite tasty for a pig.'

'Yes. He is.' I smiled, tried to remember his face at dawn.

Bella looked at her watch. 'Christ, I've got to get down and make a statement. Will you come back later tonight?' I nodded. 'I guess I could use some female company.'

'It's the shock Bella. The tears will come by the morning.'

'No, I don't think so. To be quite honest, I wasn't in love with Carlo, hadn't been for a long time. It wasn't easy to live with his despair. My inspiration fizzled out with Carlo around.'

'Then why call me, Bella, if not for comfort?'

She laughed, threw back her black tangled hair over her shoulders and sparkled her eyes.

'Because I wanted you to have the story first, Gaby. Haven't I always put sensationalism *before* respect?'

I went to Rimsky's Bar in Soho to find Deanna Stone; she usually drank champagne cocktails at six before heading for Ralph's Putney ranch. If Ralph had been off-loading smack on Carlo again I wanted him wrapped, and I wanted Kale to know that I wasn't just a second-rate journalist. He'd asked me to find the pusher, I knew Ralph was the most likely person.

I hadn't seen Deanna for several months but she walked in with the same spiky blonde hair and neatly capped teeth. I wondered if, when she carved out people's mouths, they saw the light of obsessive domination glowing in her green eyes. She greeted me with surprise, obviously she hadn't yet heard of Carlo's death.

'Gabriella, how are you! What are you doing here?'

'Looking for you.'

'You sound serious. Gravity never suited you, Gaby, is it another man, or worse?'

'Worse.'

'I was always the bravest dental student when it came to clamping jaws. Do go on, Gaby.'

We sat down and she poured me a glass of champagne. I

hated having to tell her, to be the one digging for dirt, digging for Ralph Stone.

'It's Carlo. He's dead. Overdose this afternoon. I guess Ralph knows by now. I didn't want to be the first to tell you.'

'Jesus.'

'Ralph will be upset, I know.'

'Jesus.'

She was shocked, almost tearful. I had to get to Ralph another way. 'Look, Bella's cut up too, I have to go back to Chelsea and sort her out.'

'And what about me? Didn't you know, didn't you know about *us*?'

'No, I didn't.'

'Carlo and I were having an affair. I'd got him off the hard stuff. I was sure, convinced he'd be OK. We were going to San Porella, the cure place in Spain. He was going to divorce Bella. Jesus, I called him this afternoon, I thought he was out and I left a message on his answer-machine. Oh God, Oh God . . . .'

'I put my hand on her arm, she blinked away the tears, looking at me with fear in her eyes. 'What the hell possessed him to go back on the smack?'

'It wasn't just the heroin, it seems he did it on purpose. *Who* got him the smack, that's the important thing now.'

'Ralph would. The bastard!'

'I guess there might be a bust in Putney tonight, you'd better stay somewhere else.'

She nodded, knocked back the champagne then refilled her empty glass. Deanna needed comforting but I needed to get to the truth.

'Did Bella know about you and Carlo?'

Her hands shook as she lit a thin cigar, 'She guessed I think. I used to leave weird messages on their answer-phone if he wasn't there, just to annoy her. Oh God, poor Carlo, poor Carlo!'

She was close to cracking up, but I had to dig deeper, 'And you left a message this afternoon?'

'Yes, I said something silly like, it's Deanna, how about dinner next week, sorry I missed you.'

'How odd, Bella never mentioned it.'

'It's irrelevant, isn't it?' She wiped her tear-stained face.

'Yes, I suppose so.' But I wasn't totally convinced.

I went straight back to Bella's flat. She'd given me the spare key, in case I got there first. Just my intention. It was still hot, stickier as the afternoon turned to evening. I looked up at the penthouse suite where Bella had her private studio now. No more shared warehouses, Bella insisted that art was found nearer the heavens, closer to the universe; what the hell difference did a hundred feet make?

Ralph Stone was getting out of his Porsche as I let myself into the mansion flats.

'Hey, wait for me, Gaby. Isn't Bella back yet?' He was hot, sweating like a pig in a slaughterhouse, and smelt of stale tobacco and run-down pubs full of addicts and pushers. I wondered how soon Kale would be poking around Ralph's backyard for dope.

'No. She's down at the cop-shop. Very brazen, very brave of you to appear here, Ralph. What *has* possessed you — Bella's widowhood?'

We shared the lift and Ralph pretended he cared about Carlo.

'Poor Carlo, poor man, he really was a sucker.'

'Jesus, Ralph! You've been taking that guy for rides all along the way. Did you have to find him the smack, did you have to care that much?'

'Believe me, Gaby, I didn't get it for him. Maybe in the past, OK, but not recently, not today, not me! The guy hasn't been suicidal as far as I know, so what's the big drug squad stuff, what's the accusation?'

We were in the flat, the chalk had been trampled into the carpet so Ralph didn't notice it. But I still felt that ghastly sense of recent death. I made some coffee and Ralph helped himself to the whisky.

'OK, Gaby, come on, tell me!'

'He wrote a note, suicide it appears. But he got out of the bath — as if something or someone *made* him. And why the hell did he stop to write that note?'

Ralph laughed. 'Carlo was a nut, that's why, Gaby.'

I changed the subject, the answer-machine was humming suggestively at me and I wanted to get rid of Ralph.

'Look, Bella said she wanted me to stay this evening. Why don't you come back later, Ralph? Go and look after Deanna.'

'D's tough. Hell, I know she was kinda soppy about Carlo but love isn't her style. She married me for my money. Carlo was just a childless woman's fantasy. She got him off the heroin, *he* was her child.'

The phone rang. I picked it up first. Ralph shrugged his shoulders and turned to the cocktail cabinet. I sat down beside the chalk-mark of Carlo's death pose and listened to Kale. I used to spend a lot of my time listening to Kale on the phone, wishing his job would stick itself up its own arse.

'You there again, Gaby?'

'Yes. Waiting for Bella.'

'*And* Ralph Stone?'

'How did you know?'

'We only found a couple of grammes of coke in Carlo's desk. Been looking for the hard stuff up in Bella's studio, but of course it's clean. Saw you both arrive from the window. Keep him there for a while will you?'

'For you, Kale, anything.'

'Dinner tonight?'

'No way.' And I put the phone down.

'I have to split,' said Ralph suddenly.

'Why?'

'If the pigs are going to bust my place, sweetheart, I'd rather be there to protect the bronze Buddha, don't you agree?' He kissed my cheek and there was little I could do to stop him. Kale would tease me, but at least now I had the chance to listen to that answer-machine, time to snoop around the bathtub and work out what the hell it was that was bugging me.

I turned on the answer-machine and played back the message from Deanna: 'Hi, it's Deanna, Carlo. Sorry I missed you and Bella. How about dinner, the four of us, Wednesday? Bye,' and the necessary click.

If Carlo had been half-bombed in the bath, had heard the phone ring, hadn't reached the phone in time to answer it, wouldn't that be a damned good explanation for his dripping torso across the Persian rug? But again, why the note, what the hell had he been up to? I had to talk to Kale, find out what he thought, whether the note was genuine and how much smack Carlo had actually taken. Everything was wrong.

There was a rattle of keys and Bella floated like a sylph into

the drawing room. She collapsed on to the sofa beside me just
as I was about to call my office.

'My God, darling, morgues, cop-shops! Hell they're so
sinister, so uninspiring, so bleak!'

'Look, Bella, I've got to be frank, did you know about
Deanna and Carlo, did you know they were going to Spain?'

'Has Kale Lambert been chasing you again?'

'I smiled. 'Bella, just tell me if you knew?'

She walked over to the shuttered window, London was
damp and deadly in the August heatwave, there was a frown
upon her face, her attention far away in Ralph Stone's bed.

'Yes. Will it make any difference?'

'Not now. Listen I have to call my office, I'm late. My
number at the paper – it was the last number you called wasn't
it?' I pressed the redial button, my phone number would still
be in the memory.

'Yeah, sure, police first, you last . . . . I mean I tried to care
about Carlo but he wanted to be cured of everything, drink,
fags, even sex . . . .'

I wasn't really listening to Bella. The phone clicked through
but it wasn't to my office, it wasn't to the newspaper at all, it
wasn't even to the police, it was to Deanna Stone's dental
practice. I put the phone down, confused.

'You didn't call Deanna did you?'

'Of course not, darling, why should I, nobody made any
calls, not even Lambert's band.'

I dialled my number and spoke briefly to Bug, the news-desk
editor. Bella stood at the window still speculating on life,
creativity and Carlo's tragic death.

'And of course Ralph will keep the business going, he might
even marry me one day. Well, you've always known that,
haven't you, Gaby?'

'Yes, yes, I . . .'

There was a knock on the door. It was Kale. There was a
faint glint of ridicule on his face, my earlier blanking of his
dinner proposal hadn't apparently affected his nauseous pride.

'Your studio's clean, Bella. But you ought to know that
Ralph will probably be hauled in for pushing heroin; it's the
way Carlo probably got it if that's any consolation.'

He lit a cigarette as Bella looked down at the chalk on the

rug and began to brush it away with her blood-red fingernails. 'No it's not, Detective Lambert, no it's not!'

'They're lovers,' I said as if the whole world except Kale Lambert knew.

'How inconvenient,' was all he said, but he looked at me and nodded and I followed him out into the stairwell.

'You staying, Gaby?'

'For a while. There's something I need to find out about Carlo's death.'

'Like what?'

'I don't think it was suicide.'

'Then what?'

'A kind of murder.'

'Difficult to prove, Gaby, no motive, no weapons, no evidence.'

'Oh come on, Kale, it's all there! It's smack, smack's the weapon, smack's the motive, smack's the evidence! And there are other things, a phone call to Deanna, you lot didn't make one, Bella says she didn't. Jesus, Kale, aren't you suspicious?'

'I'll be at Rimsky's for dinner at ten, if you're interested, Gaby.'

'Carlo's death, that's what interests me, not your dining arrangements!'

The lift door opened and shut on his laughing face. There was never any way of getting through to Kale Lambert, never had been. And it was then, suddenly, that I understood. That I knew what must have happened to poor Carlo Reeves.

Bella had opened a bottle of Burgundy when I walked back into the drawing room. God, she was cool, that remote, brilliant talent of art-school days had been put to a different use. Her craft was pretence now, not art.

I said slowly, 'Bella, look, I've got to tell you – I think Carlo was killed by a lethal overdose he wasn't expecting. I think it was murder.'

'How grotesque, Gaby, how bizarre. This could be your biggest story yet, do enlighten me, darling.'

'It's all to do with the telephone. You told me I was the last person you phoned when you found Carlo dead. I think I was, but you weren't *here* in the flat, you were in the studio upstairs.'

'Hell, Gabs, what does that prove?'

'It means you probably rang me and the police *before* you got down here, which really seems to imply that you *knew* Carlo would be dead.'

'How absurd.' She poked her delicate fingers into the Persian rug, eyes away from me, the chalk almost gone.

'Not really. It's your damned sensationalist, impatient mind Bella, you thrive on it!'

'Go on.'

'There was something that struck me as similar about Carlo's note and Deanna's answer-machine message. Both illogical, both not quite what they were meant to be. And then, when I phoned my office I pressed the redial button, because you told me my number was the last number you called. It was, but not on *this* phone. *You* called me from the studio, the last number dialled on the phone here in the flat was Deanna Stone's!'

'And?'

'I'm just guessing, but I think the phone rang when Carlo was already spaced out in the bath, dying. It was Deanna, he tried to answer it but didn't get there in time. But she had left a message, on the answer-machine. He was feeling high, coming down, who knows, so he tried to call Deanna back. She was probably engaged so he kept trying until he finally gave up and started to write a note to her, knowing he was going to chase the dragon. The note said, "I can't get through . . ." – I think he meant he couldn't *get through* on the telephone. It just happened to be a lucky bonus, that note, it helped to make Carlo's murder look like suicide.'

'Very ingenious, Gaby, but I had no reason to kill him, none at all.'

'But Deanna did, didn't she?'

Bella sighed. All the chalk had been rubbed away; there was no more Carlo, no more point in pretending. 'Deanna was tired of their affair. She didn't like the burden of being Carlo's saviour, wanted to set up a practice in the States or something. She knew how much Ralph and I wanted to be together so she asked me to help her encourage Carlo to an early grave. She'd bugger off to the States and leave Ralph with no hard feelings.'

'Who gave Carlo the smack?'

'I suppose I gave it to him. Deanna gave it to me and told me to dangle it under his nose. "Once a junkie, always a junkie," she said. "One snort to hell, that's all you needed with that stuff." She said it was lethal. I told Carlo Deanna and Ralph had made it up and were off to Marbella for the summer, it was easy. He couldn't cope with that. God how he loved her! The jealous, broken sod grabbed the packet out of my hand and I left the flat and headed for the studio. Deanna said he'd be dead by four o'clock. She rang to check, but she left that stupid message – God he must have been confused!'

'No doubt when he tried to call her back she was on the phone to you, Bella, telling *you* he was dead.'

I stood up, smiled, not through smugness, just pity and an unstoppable relief.

'I think you might be famous at last, Bella, even if it is an ephemeral blaze of passion!'

At Rimsky's Bar Kale sat, back turned to the door as I stepped off the damp streets of a drizzling summer night. I was surprised he was still there, surprised he had ever expected me to show up. Earlier I had had little intention of doing so, but now I had a prize for him. He could have Ralph Stone for pushing smack and Deanna Stone for murder, maybe Bella too.

'It *was* Deanna's scam, but try the bronze Buddha at Ralph's ranch; just a hunch, I think he keeps all that lethal dope stashed away in it.' I flopped down opposite him and he handed me a glass of champagne. 'Drinking on duty, Kale, tut tut, you're slipping, or business is bad.'

'It's just dirty Gaby, not bad. You always knew that. But I'll admit you beat me to it if that's what you came to hear.'

'No.'

'And you're goddamned ambiguous.'

I laughed. 'Not in print, not in the morning I won't be.'

'Nobody cared about Carlo very much did they, Gaby?'

'I did. Hell, I should have known Deanna was dangerous. She always did stop crying once the heads were ripped off the sardines.'

'Stay for another bottle?'

I kissed his cheek quickly. 'Another time, Kale, I've got a deadline to catch.'

'So had Carlo Reeves.'

DANGEROUS SPORT

CELIA FREMLIN

Celia Fremlin was educated at Berkhamsted School for Girls and at Somerville College, Oxford. She spent the War working for Mass Observation during the day, and for the local A.R.P. service during the night. She married Dr. E.S. Goller in 1943, and began her writing career a decade or so later. Her first novel, *The Hours Before Dawn*, was awarded an Edgar by the Mystery Writers of America.

She lives in London in an old house overlooking Hampstead Heath, has two children and two grandchildren, and when not writing novels, works as a charwoman locally.

Dangerous Sport appeared in *Ellery Queen's Mystery Magazine*.

'Darling, I'd just love to be able to stay a bit longer. You know I would. I'm just as disappointed as you are. But . . . .'

But.

But, but, but. What would it be *this* time, Stella wondered sourly? Whatever it was, she'd have heard it before, that was certain. After five years of going around with a married man, a girl knows his repertoire by heart.

But I have to help Wendy with the week-end shopping. *But* the man is coming to do the boiler. *But* I have to fetch Carol from the Brownies. *But* Simon is away from school with a temperature. *But* I have to meet Aunt Esmé at the airport.

This last had been the funniest one of all. Looking back, Stella could hardly help laughing, in a black, bitter sort of way, though at the time it hadn't seemed funny at all. For it had come so soon – so cruelly, and (as it turned out) so ironically soon after that golden September day when, lying in the long

60

grass by the river beyond Marlow, Gerald had been confiding in her, as married men will, about the depth of his inner loneliness. Even as a child he'd been lonely, it seemed.

'No brothers or sisters. Not even any uncles or aunts,' he'd explained sadly. 'I used to long, sometimes, for one of those big, close, quarrelsome families, all weddings and funerals and eating roast chicken and bread sauce at each other's tables, and running down each other's in-laws. I yearned for something beyond the tight, nuclear family in which I was raised – just myself and my two parents. I'd have given anything for a disapproving aunt or two, or a black-sheep uncle! Particularly at Christmas I used to feel . . . .'

Stella couldn't remember, at this distance of time, what the hell it was that Gerald used to feel at Christmas: something about tangerines, and somebody else's grandfather out in the snow sawing apple-logs – or something – it was of no importance, which of course was why she'd forgotten it. What *was* important, and she wouldn't forget it till her dying day, was the discrepancy she'd instantly spotted between those maudlin reminiscences and the cock-and-bull story, only three months later, about having to meet 'Aunt Esmé' at the airport.

No brothers or sisters. Poor, lonely little boy with no aunts or uncles, even. And so who the hell *was* this 'Aunt Esmé'?

She'd given him every chance. Why couldn't *Wendy* be the one to meet the woman, she'd asked, watching him intently while she spoke? After all, she was Wendy's aunt, not his . . . . 'Oh, no, darling, no, whatever gave you that idea, she's *my* aunt, she was awfully good to me as a kid, and so I feel that this is the least I can do. It's an awful bore, but . . . . You *do* understand, don't you, darling?'

Of course she'd understood. That's what mistresses are for.

'*Of course*, darling!' she'd said, not batting an eyelid; and afterwards, how she'd laughed about it, when she'd finished crying.

She had to be so very careful, that was the thing: call Gerald's bluff even once, and the whole thing could have been wrecked for ever. He had made it quite, quite clear to her, very early on in the relationship, that suspicion, jealousy and possessiveness were the prerogative of the wife, and of the wife alone. It was in the nature of things (Gerald seemed to feel) that *Wendy* should cross-question him about his business trips, ring up the office to check that he really was working late, go through his pockets for letters and for incriminating theatre-ticket stubs: but for *Stella* to do these things struck him as an outrage, an insult to the natural order of things.

'Look, darling,' he'd said (and the cold savagery of his tone had seemed to Stella quite out of proportion to her very minor misdemeanour – a single tentative little phone call to his secretary asking – just simply asking – what time he was expected back from Wolverhampton). 'Look, darling, when a married man starts an affair, it's because he wants to get *away* from this sort of thing, not because he wants more of it. He has enough trouble getting a few hours' freedom as it is, without having his mistress waiting for him like a cat at a mousehole every time he steps outside his front door!'

A speech both cruel and uncalled-for, and Stella had been dreadfully upset. But being upset never got you anywhere with Gerald, it just made him avoid answering the telephone; and so after a while she'd stopped being upset, and had resolved to watch her step even more carefully in the future. And so this was why, when the Aunt Esmé thing cropped up, she'd let it pass without a flicker of protest. Dumber than the dumbest blonde she'd been, as she sleeked back her wings of black, burnished hair, and listened, her dark eyes wide and trusting, while he floundered deeper and deeper into a labyrinth of lies and evasions from which he would never (unless she, Stella, chose to assist him) be able to extricate himself.

For the lies hadn't ended with meeting 'Aunt Esmé' at the airport, they had gone on for weeks. Because that hypothetical lady's visit had proved to be a long one, and packed with incident. She had to be taken to the theatre on just the night when Gerald usually went out with Stella; she caught flu on the exact weekend when Gerald and Stella had planned a trip to the country; and when Stella herself caught flu, she had to have it alone because it just so happened that Aunt Esmé had to be taken on a visit to an old school-friend in Bournemouth at just that time.

And Stella had taken it all, smiling. Smiling, smiling endlessly down the telephone, making understanding noises, and never questioning, never protesting. It had been over a year later (surely a *year* is long enough? Surely no one could accuse you of checking-up after a *year*?) before Stella had ventured, warily, and with lowered eyelids, to ask after Aunt Esmé. Had they seen her lately, or had a card from her, she'd asked innocently, one láte December day when Gerald, preoccupied, brimming-over with family life, had driven over hastily with Stella's present. Jewellery again, and expensive. Gerald was good at this sort of thing.

Stella thanked him prettily, even warmly; and then, still prettily, she tossed her bombshell into his face.

'Have you heard from Aunt Esmé lately?' she asked, and enjoyed, as she only rarely enjoyed his love-making, the look of blank, uncomplicated bewilderment that overspread his pink, self-satisfied features. Not even any wariness, so completely had he forgotten the whole thing.

'Aunt Esmé? Who's Aunt Esmé?' he asked curiously, quite unsuspicious.

Stella had intended it to stop there: to brush it off with a light, 'Oh, well, I must be mixing it up with some other family'; to leave him unscathed, untouched by guilt, and to savour her triumph in secret. But the temptation to go on, to spring the trap, was irresistible.

'Aunt Esmé, darling! You know – the one you had staying with you for all that time last winter . . . ,' and as she spoke Stella watched, with terror and with glee, the dawning of guilt and alarm in his bland, contented features. Fear, calculation and panic darted like fishes back and forth across his plump countenance; and then he recovered himself.

Of course! How stupid! Dear old *Esmé*, you must mean! Not an aunt at all, but the old family governess from Wendy's mother's old home . . . the children had been taught to call her 'aunt' because, well, because, you know . . . .

And of course Stella *did* know; smiling, and lying, and letting him off the hook. She, too, had had an 'aunt' like that in her childhood. An Aunt Polly, she hastily improvised, who had made gingerbread animals . . . . Smiling, inventing, chattering, easing the thing, Stella was nevertheless already making her plans. In a year's time – or maybe two years – 'How's your mother-in-law's old governess getting on?' she'd ask, all innocence, watching his face while he blundered into the trap:

'*Governess?* But Wendy's mother never had ...' And while his words stuttered into silence, she would be watching his face, never taking her eyes off it as it disintegrated into terror, bewilderment and guilt.

Guilt, that was the important thing. Guilt, so richly deserved and so long outstanding, like an unpaid debt. Such a sense of power it gave her to be able to call him to account like this, just now and again; a sense of power which compensated, in some measure, for the awful weakness of her actual position, the terrible uncertainty about her hold on him. To be able to make him squirm like this, every so often, was a sort of redressing of some desperate balance; a long-merited turning of the tables without which Stella sometimes felt she could not have gone on.

Oh, but it was fun, too! A sort of game of Catch-me-if-you-can, a fun game. Not quite so much fun, though, as it used to be, because of late Gerald had been growing more wary, less easily trapped. He was more evasive now, less buoyantly ready to come out with give-away remarks like '*What* trip to Manchester, darling?' or, 'But they've never *had* measles ....' Now, before he spoke, you could see him checking through the lies he had told recently, his grey-green eyes remote and sly.

And as Gerald grew more wary, so did Stella grow more cunning. The questions by which she trapped him were never direct ones now, but infinitely subtle and devious. It was a dangerous sport, and like all dangerous sports, it demanded skill and judgment, a sure eye and perfect timing. Push Gerald too far, and she would have a terrible, terrifying row on her hands – 'Possessive!' 'Demanding!' and all the other age-old accusations hurtling round her head. Push him not far enough, however, and the opposite set of mishaps would be set in train. He would start thinking he could get away with anything ... leaving her for days on end without so much as a phone call, and then turning up all smiles, as if nothing had happened, and expecting her to cook him steak and collect his shoes from the repairers. Taking her for granted, just as if she was a wife: and what sensible woman is going to put up with all the dis-advantages of being married *as well as* all the disadvantages of not being?

It was a cliff-hanger business, getting the thing exactly right. Only a few months ago, Gerald had actually threatened to leave her if she didn't stop spying on him – though surely 'spying' was unduly harsh a term to apply to Stella's innocent little show of interest in the details of the business conference he'd pretended he'd been to the previous weekend?

'But, darling, Lord Berners wasn't *at* the dinner!' she'd pointed out, with a placating little laugh, just to save Gerald the trouble of inventing any more humorous quotes from a non-existent speech, 'I read in *The Times* the next morning that . . .' – and at this, quite suddenly, he had gone berserk, and had turned on her like an animal at bay. His rage, his dreadful, unwarrantable accusations, were like nothing she had ever heard before, and they threw her into such terror that she scarcely knew what she was doing or saying. In the end, he had flung himself out of the flat, slamming the door on her tears and screams, and vowing never to set foot in the place again.

It had taken a suicide note, no less, to bring him to heel again. It was just about as generous a suicide note as any woman ever penned to a recalcitrant lover, and Stella still remembered it with a certain measure of satisfaction, despite the misery appertaining to its composition.

'You mustn't blame yourself, darling,' she'd written, 'it is my decision, and mine alone. If I cannot face life without you, that is *my* problem, not yours. So don't, my love, feel that you have to come rushing round when you get this letter; the very last thing I want – or have ever wanted – is to inconvenience you in any way, or make you feel guilty. Anyway, by the time you get this, it will be too late. By then, I shall already . . . .'

The posts must have been slow that week, because it was nearly three days before she'd at last heard his feet pounding up the stairs, and had started taking the pills, stuffing them into her mouth in handfuls as he burst into the room.

It had been worth it, though. He'd been sweet to her for days afterwards, visiting her constantly in hospital, and even after she'd got home, he'd continued to shower her with flowers and presents, calling nearly every day, and displaying in full measure the remorse, the tenderness, and the self-recrimination that such a situation demands of a man.

Until, of course, he got bored with it. First bored, and then resentful. 'Blackmail' he called it now whenever Stella tried to get him to do anything he didn't want: and Stella began to realise, gradually, that she was right back at square one: having to be careful . . . careful. The only way she could hold him now was by avoiding occasions for quarrels, and by being infinitely tolerant and understanding: in short, by letting him get away with every bloody thing.

And so this was why, this summer Saturday afternoon, Stella, her teeth set in a smile, was making herself listen without a murmur to what Gerald was saying. She had known, of course, the *kind* of thing it would be; married men always have such *righteous* reasons for letting you down. Sick wives – kids home on holiday – family visits: all perfectly uncheckable, and all showing up what a kind, compassionate, virtuous, dutiful creature the lying, treacherous creature is.

Well, and so what was it *this* time?

Simon's Sports Day. Gerald was potty about that kid.

'You *do* understand, don't you, darling?' he was pleading; and of course she understood very well. Understood that he preferred the prospect of watching a nine-year-old running across a field in gym shoes, to the prospect of spending a whole long afternoon with his mistress, cool and mysterious in her darkened flat, the sunlight flickering across the bed through the slatted blinds . . . .

'You see, darling, the thing is, he might *win*! Only nine-and-a-half, and he might actually *win* the under-eleven two hundred and twenty yards! He's a marvellous little runner, Mr Foulkes tells me, he has a real athlete's body!'

A real athlete's body. The light shining in Gerald's eyes was something Stella had never seen before, not even at the height of their love-making. For a few seconds, she tried to imagine what it would be like to be the mother of that small athlete's body, to have produced it jointly with Gerald; to have a right, now, to share in that idiot pride . . . . At the sight of those heavy, self-indulgent features thus irradiated, Stella felt a great darkness coming around her. It came like a black, monstrous wave, engulfing her, leaving her bereft of speech.

'I wouldn't miss it for a million pounds!' she heard him saying, from somewhere outside the swirling blackness. 'To hear his name called – "Simon Graves" – my own son! And then the clapping . . . the cheers . . . ! And him only nine-and-a-half! The others are all over ten, darling, *all* of them! He's the only nine-year-old who managed to . . . .'

She preferred his lies: preferred them a thousand times. How could she have guessed that the truth, when she finally heard it from those evasive, prevaricating lips, would hurt as much as this?

The school gates were propped wide open and welcoming, and through them, in the blazing sunshine, trooped the mothers and the fathers; the sisters and the girl-friends and the aunts. With their white sandals, their bright summer dresses or pale, freshly-ironed slacks, women just like Stella, somewhere vaguely in their thirties, were thick upon the ground. Among so many, who was going to give her a second glance? Unless, of course, she gave herself away somehow – walking too fast, maybe, or letting her eyes flit too purposefully this way and that?

The fathers were altogether less numerous than their womenfolk, which made Stella's task that much easier: they stuck out among the bright dresses like the dark stumps of trees. Stella's eyes darted from one to another of them ceaselessly, for he might be *anywhere*; and supposing – just *supposing* – he were to catch sight of her before she'd managed to locate *him*!

Not a big risk, really. For she had the advantage that the hunter always has over the prey – she knew what she was looking for, and what she meant to do when she found it; whereas Gerald not only wasn't on the watch for her – he hadn't the slightest suspicion that she could possibly be here at all. On top of which she had, after a fashion, disguised herself with a pair of large round sunglasses and a white silk bandanna wound tightly round her black, shining hair.

Across the lawn . . . up under the avenue of limes the slow procession wound, all chattering, exclaiming, exchanging greetings; some were already fanning themselves against the heat. Slowly likewise, but with heart hammering, Stella matched her pace with the rest; and it was not until she had settled herself on the grass at the far end of a long line of deckchairs facing the sports field that she began to breathe more easily. Hemmed-in by all these chairs, she could scarcely be seen from more than a yard or two away, and yet by craning her neck she could still get a good view of the crowds still winding up from the school buildings. Here and there a dark head, taller than the rest, would make her catch her breath; but always, it was a false alarm.

And now here was the junior P.E. master walking up and down with his loud-hailer, announcing the order of events. Already, the crowd was falling into an expectant silence, the thousand voices dying away in wave after wave, fading away like the twitter of birds at twilight.

And still Gerald hadn't come.

Had he been lying to her after all? Had his afternoon's truancy had nothing to do with Simon's Sports Day, in spite of all those passionate declarations of paternal pride? The swine! The double-crossing, treacherous swine! All that emotion wasted – not to mention having let herself in for a long, hot afternoon of boredom, all for nothing!

I'll teach you, Gerald Graves! I'll teach you to lie to me, make a fool of me! Thought you'd get away with it, didn't you – *I'll* show you . . . !

Already, she could feel a line of sweat gathering under the bandanna, along her hair-line. She'd never worn such a thing before, and by God, she thought, I never will again!

Under-sixteen hurdles . . . .'

'Quarter mile, under fourteen . . . .'

The sheer tedium of it was beginning to make Stella feel quite ill; her back ached, her eyes ached, and her brain felt half-addled with heat and boredom.

Long jump. High jump . . . . On and on the thing droned; whistles blew, shouts exploded into the shimmering air and died away again; the clapping and the cheering rose and fell, and rose again. Cup for this . . . . Prize for that . . . . The sun beat down, the voices swelled and receded . . . and then, just when Stella was on the verge of sleep, she heard it.

'Simon Graves! Winner of the under-eleven two hundred and twenty yards! Simon Graves!'

Stella was sitting bolt upright now, peering past the forest of chairs to get a glimpse of the sports field; but before she had time to locate the dark-haired little boy scuttling proudly towards the side-lines, she became aware of a small commotion going on in front of her and a few yards to the right.

'*Simon!* Our Simon! He's *done* it, Mummy! Daddy said he would! Oh, Simon . . . Si-i-imon!'

'Hush, darling, hush Carol, you must sit down . . . .' A plumpish, smiling woman was pulling at the sleeve of a wildly gesticulating little girl of about seven, urging her back into her seat. 'Hush, Carol darling, not so loud, Simon'll be embarrassed. Oh, but won't Daddy be pleased!'

'Daddy will say . . . .' 'Daddy will think . . . .' And where the hell *is* Daddy, if one might enquire? 'Wouldn't miss it for a million pounds,' he'd said. Someone, somewhere, with more than a million pounds to spare this bright afternoon?

Peering between the lines of chairs, Stella could see that the exultant mother and little sister were about to receive their hero. Pounding up the bank he came, wiry and brown and all lit-up with triumph, hurling himself upon his mother and sister amid a babble of congratulations from all around.

Past the chairs, past the stirring, smiling people, Stella watched, and kept very still. What *right* had the three of them to such joy, such total, undiluted happiness? Did they not know that the foundations of it were rotten – that their cosy little family life was based on a rotting, disintegrating substructure of lies and cheating? 'Daddy this . . .' and 'Daddy that . . .'. It made her quite sick to listen to the shrill little voices filled with such baseless adoration.

Quietly, unobtrusively, Stella got to her feet, and worked her way along between the rows of chairs. She reached the little girl just when mother and brother had turned away for a moment, receiving further congratulations. Quickly, Stella dropped on her knees in front of the child, bringing their faces level.

'Do you know why your Daddy isn't here?' she said softly, 'It's because he's spent the afternoon in bed with me! *In bed.* Do you understand?'

The blank, stupid look on the child's face maddened her. She leaned closer.

'In *bed*! Having *sex*!' she hissed. 'Sex, sex, sex! Don't you know what sex is? Don't they give you Sex Education at the bloody Brownies or somewhere?'

The blank look was still on the child's face to the end. But Stella had the satisfaction – after she had squeezed back past row after row of chairs and had almost escaped from the enclosure – of hearing Carol, at last, burst into loud sobbing.

It was nearly ten o'clock when, at long last, she heard Gerald's step on the stairs; and even after all these hours, she still could not have said whether she'd been expecting him to come, or to stay away.

He'd be angry, of course. But also, surely relieved? Five years of secrecy was too much; it would be a relief to everyone to have it out in the open.

'Don't you agree, darling, that it was high time we had it out in the open?' she was asking, for the fourth or fifth time, of the silent, slumped figure in the arm-chair. She'd been trying ever since his arrival to extract some sort of response from him. She'd tried everything – even congratulating him on his son's success.

'Pity you weren't there to see it,' she'd been unable to resist adding; but even this had provoked from Gerald nothing more than the bald, factual statement that he *had* seen it, thank you, from the Pavilion, where some of the fathers were helping to organise the boys.

Then more silence. She tried again.

'I'm sorry, Gerald darling, if Carol – if the little girl – was upset. I didn't mean to upset her, I just thought that the children should know about us. I don't believe in lies and deceit with children, I think they are entitled to the truth. Oh, darling, please don't look like that! It's been a shock, I know, but I'm sure that when you've had time to think about it, you'll see it's been all for the best. The best for *us*, and for Wendy, too. She can't have liked all this lying and deception all these years. I'm sure she'd rather know where she stands, and be able to start making sensible plans for the future. I mean, she looks quite a nice sort of person, I don't think she'll make any trouble once she understands that we love each other. Oh, darling, what *is* it? Why don't you *say* something? Look, let's have a drink and relax, and think what we're going to do when the unpleasantness is over. This flat is a bit small for the two of us, but assuming that you'll be getting half the value of your house, then between us we could . . . '

And now, at last, he *did* make a move. He rose, stiffly, and she thought that he was about to pour each of them a large glass of whisky. Instead, he walked over to the table in the window where Stella's typewriter stood, open. Laboriously, with one finger, he began to type.

Stella left it a minute – two minutes – and then walked over to look.

> 'Gerald B. Graves
>   27 Firfield Gardens,
>   Sydenham Way . . .'

The long manilla envelope stared up at her from the typewriter carriage. She watched, stupefied, while he finished the last few letters of the address. Then –

'Whatever are you doing, darling?' she asked, with an uneasy little laugh. 'Are you writing a letter to *yourself* . . . ?'

And then she saw it, just by his right hand. Her own suicide note of last autumn – 'By the time you get this, darling, I shall be dead . . . .'

'The handwriting will be unquestionably yours,' he observed conversationally. 'And the address will have been typed on your typewriter. The postmark will also be right, as I shall post it myself, on my way out. It should reach me at breakfast time the day after tomorrow, just in time to show to the police. And now, my dear, just one more little job, and we shall be finished.'

And as he stood up and turned towards her, the light from the lamp fell full on his face, and she saw the look in his eyes.

'No . . . no . . . !' she gasped, took a step backwards, and shrank, whimpering, against the wall.

'I intend it to look like suicide,' he said, as if reassuring her;

71

and as he moved across the carpet towards her, Stella's last coherent thought was: He will, too! He'll get away with it, he'll lie his way out of it, just as he's always done.

How accomplished a liar he was, she, of course, knew better than anyone, for it was she who had trained him; trained him, like a circus animal, over five long years.

BOX

ZEBA KALIM

Zeba Kalim was born in Cambridge in 1964. She was educated in the USA and Britain and has worked in the City of London and in publishing.

I could sense him waiting for me outside the shop. Watching me again. I didn't have to turn, I knew he was there. I gripped the counter so tight that my fingers were numb when it came to taking the next customer's books and cashing them up at the till. I fumbled and the pile of paperbacks slipped but I caught them before they fell to the floor and smiled, nervously, I suppose, at the woman. She grinned, anyway, saying, 'One of those days?' but she sighed when I muffed the prices and had to start keying them in all over again. Why had she bought so many books anyway? Once I'd wrestled them into a carrier, I gripped the counter again, waiting for her to write the cheque, but she took forever. She was left-handed and the light bounced off a diamond ring squeezed on to her fourth finger as she carefully formed every letter, just like a little kid at school. I got really impatient and looked away, out of the window, and there he was, just as I knew he would be.

'What's the . . . are you all right, love?' The woman's voice made me jump.

'The date is the twelfth of March.'

That wiped the concern away quick enough. I took her cheque card and wrote the number on the back smartly, but I nearly handed her back the cheque with the card and the receipt. She left quickly, her eyebrows shrugging me off her mind. I wondered whether the police would trace her as a witness. What for? All she'd seen was a stroppy salesgirl.

The bell rang as the door shut behind her. She was the last person from the tea-time rush. Would he come in? I wished the shop were modern, with video cameras or something. Why had I said I'd lock up? I knew he'd be there. But it was my turn, I couldn't get out of it. And what was I frightened of anyway? I'm a big girl, my dad calls me a strapping lass, my brothers call me Thunderthighs, but I retaliate, I call them – oh, it doesn't matter, I can tell he's still there, and he'll try to talk to me on the way home, and follow me, walking a few paces behind me along the edge of the Common, those pale eyes boring into my back, I don't normally notice eyes, but I know his all right.

He didn't come into the shop, he didn't have to, I could feel him there, every time I turned as I went around straightening the stock, dusting the shelves. I hadn't minded being chatted up first of all, it had been a lark, I don't often get chatted up, being large and all. It was nice to meet someone new, a fella who was taller and broader than me, all sexy too in his Levis and his leather jacket. His hair is really dark and his eyes are yellow, like lamps, really light. Unusual. Unforgettable. And now they're trained on me like searchlights on a prison camp.

I tried to tell my mate Carol, but she thought I was making him up to keep up with the rest of the crowd. God I wish I were, I wish he was just imaginary, that I could just switch him off like the telly. He wanted me to go out with him, but I wouldn't, especially not after he'd told me about the slaughterhouse.

'I'm an artiste of the abattoir. I slice up pigs and cows and sheep. Sometimes I wish I was slitting throats of something else too, know what I mean, love?' he said, turning those headlamp eyes on me, smiling.

Maybe he didn't hear me say no, the first time he asked me out, but he got the message when I didn't answer his questions all right. But he kept on meeting me at the Common when I got off the bus, even when I wouldn't talk. He'd talk to me, tell me all about slicing up the animals, skinning them and hacking at their vertebrae, sawing off their trotters. He brought me a sheep's hoof, all bloody, thrust it into my hand and suddenly I could smell the fear of those animals, herded together, lined up, ready for their knocks on the chump, or injections on the rump, watching as the one in front crumpled.

'Keep it safe, love, nice and safe to remind you of me.'

I walked on, not looking at him, my eyes fixed on the path, if I looked away, I'd be lost. He let me go, watched me out of sight, chuckling. When I turned the corner, I hurled that bone into the first skip I found, but he knew that too, and my hand was all bloody from gripping it.

My mum couldn't understand why I wouldn't eat meat any more and muttered at me over mealtimes, especially the Sunday roast, when Paul, my biggest brother came home with his wife Linda, she was a right bitch, she kept up a running commentary about faddy eaters and how Mum should keep my dinner and serve it up to me every meal until I ate it. Dad patted my hand and took my food, but the sound of it squelching round his gums revolted me, I burst into tears and ran upstairs and I could hear Paul yelling, 'Now look what you've done, you stupid cow.'

So he was there too, and I cried again because I began to understand that I'd never get away from him or his neat white hands that held sharp knives of different shapes every day.

Then he didn't turn up at the Common for a bit, and at first that was great, I was free, but then I began to catch glimpses of him, in the street, watching my face as the bus flashed past on the way to work. He's got this bike, really fancy, and once he just kept up at the side of the bus, watching me, smiling as I looked at him, laughing when the bus stopped and he whizzed on. Sometimes I see him when I'm out shopping, just his reflection in a shop window, still, while everybody is dashing around. I saw him standing opposite the sandwich bar where me and my mates go for lunch, so I gave up lunch, just sat in the kitchen over the shop, the Staff Room, as Mr Melksham calls it. Some bloody staff, there's Melky and old Miss La-di-da Barnes and yours truly stuck up a bloody side street. I wish I'd taken that job at the Tescos, but Dad said I'd be better off in the bookshop, I'd learn something, it wouldn't be so boring, my prospects would be better 'cos a bookshop's got more class than a supermarket. All my mates went into the Tescos or Woollies on the High Street though, or they're on the dole, and they all go out on Saturdays, down to the Plough or the Blue Box. I don't any more, because of course he'll be there. I stay at home now, watching Les Dennis and videos with

Mum. She eats all the time, crisps and pork scratchings, so all the things she knits for Linda's brat are greasy and stink of salt and vinegar. It's going to be called Kim if it's a girl, Damien if it's a boy.

An old geezer came into the shop, the sort that Barnesy would call 'a gentleman of the old school', all wrapped up. He huffed and puffed, shook the rain all over the lino as he shut his brolly and asked, 'May I leave this with you, my dear?'

I think I just nodded, I can't remember, because it was getting darker all the time and I was watching the shadows shift from street lamp to street lamp, trying to make out which one was him. I didn't notice the old chap until he called out, 'Excuse me, please, can you help me?'

I tried to put on a smile, he was being really polite, not like most people, and went over to him, he was in the back room, where Barnesy sits.

'Could you show me the poetry section? I'm looking for Dante's *Divine Comedy*.'

'He's that Italian, yeah?'

'Indeed, the poet.'

'We got it in Penguin Classics, over here.'

I led him across, but half-way I heard the bell go and jumped a mile, and the old man buffeted right into me and fell back, so I grabbed hold of him until he got his balance back.

'I was actually wondering whether you had the Oxford University Press three-volume edition with the Italian and an English translation. My granddaughter is studying English at university. She's never read Dante. I don't know what they teach in these schools nowadays. The facts of life and Contemporary Studies. No passion, no thought.'

'This it?' I pointed at the books. He looked at me hard. 'Sir?'

'Thank you so much.' I liked his smile, but the doorbell jangled again. 'Revolting covers, they clash. I don't understand why they can't print the damn thing in a single volume with an attractive jacket. No wonder people don't read it any more. I must say, I'm gratified to find you stock it. I imagined I'd have to order it.'

'It's for students, sir, at the college.' I bent down to pull them off the shelf.

'I'm glad to hear that someone somewhere studies Dante

76

now.' He took them from me and started for the cash desk. I didn't want him to go, he made me feel safe, which was daft, I could have beaten him up myself he was so doddery.

There was a box on the counter. I pushed it to one side, it wasn't very big. I cashed up the Dante, and the old man pulled out a credit card, one of those gold ones that you only get if you're richer than the Queen. While I was mucking about with the machine and the slip, he put on a pair of glasses and read out, '*L'amor che muove il sole e l'altre stelle*. The love that moves the sun and the other stars. There, that's what we need to learn about. I sign here, yes?'

After he'd gone, I locked the door. I would open it if anyone really wanted to come in, but I was petrified, of the box, of his coming in again, of the cold and the wet. I'd ring home, say I was staying over with Carol, and sleep in the shop. But first I wanted to get it over with and open the box.

I pulled it back into the centre and looked out of the window again, but I couldn't see him or anyone else. I cut the Sellotape with the scalpel Melky uses for opening parcels, and took the lid off. I separated the tissue paper and there was a hand and an ear. I slammed the lid back on again, and maybe I screamed, but maybe I only thought I did, and I turned away and retched and retched, but my stomach was empty so nothing came up. I was shivering and shaking and I heard these funny whimpering noises, and then I realised they were me and I just collapsed on to the floor and sobbed. I don't know how long it took, but I calmed down a bit and knew I couldn't stay in the shop all night alone with the box, and I was too terrified to walk out the door on my own. I looked at my watch, it was six o'clock. They'd be waiting for me at home, but if I rang and asked someone to come over to help me go back they'd laugh and say I was stupid.

I heard a siren out on the High Street, and then I thought about the rozzers. It made sense, after all, they'd want to find out whose hand and ear it was anyway, and they might even catch him, and he'd never bother me ever again, they'd lock him up. I went to the phone and dialled 999. It was strange, I'd never done it before. A girl answered, asking whether I wanted the police, an ambulance or a fire engine. I said, 'The police.' I nearly said 'All of them', and the thought made me giggle, then

I saw his face, pressed close up against the glass, squashing his nose and his chin until he looked deformed, like his face was melting. I screamed, and then I heard a man asking, 'What's the trouble, what's going on there?'

'Please, please come quick, Melksham's Bookshop, on Torrance Street, please, he's here and I'm so frightened.'

'Speak up, girl, was that Torrance Street?' I'd whispered everything so he wouldn't hear me, but the copper hadn't heard me, and his face at the window seemed to get larger and larger and I was panting now, because he was so close and the glass between us was getting thinner and thinner and dissolving away.

'Here this isn't a hoax?'

'No. No, please, please, Melksham's Bookshop,' I howled. I must have sounded a total nutter.

'It's all right, girl, just calm down and tell me what's going on.'

'He's outside, and he's going to get in, I know it, please help.'

I heard a thump at the back of the shop and I whirled around, but I couldn't see a thing, and when I turned back to the window, he'd gone. A note slipped under the door and I hung up and went round to pick it up. It was just folded up and it said in capitals:

YOU'RE NEXT LOVE.

I backed away from the door, and then I heard a noise at the back of the shop again. I wheeled and picked up the scalpel still lying on the counter where I'd left it by the box. I edged round the counter and into the corner where I could look out of the window and see into the back room by turning my head. Then I moved along the side wall, taking quick looks out the front, so that I could see all of the back room. There wasn't anything, and the back door had been locked and bolted by Melky when he left at three, there was nothing to be afraid of, there really wasn't. I went back to my perch, and waited, waited for the police. I smoothed my palms across my overall and felt a damp patch on my right thigh. I looked down, and saw that I'd cut my thumb with the scalpel and it was bleeding all over the place. It began to sting and throb, and I slipped the scalpel into my pocket and held my thumb tight, too frightened to go up to the bathroom and use the first aid kit. A drop of blood ran over my left hand and plopped on the lino, glistening on the dark green floor, spreading a little, following the slope. I sat and watched it, mesmerised and gasped when I heard a sharp rap on the door.

'Police here, you can open up now.' It was a woman's voice. The checked hatband and the dark solid shape of her reassured me.

'Wait a minute.' I don't know whether they heard me or not, but I opened the door, and in she came with her partner.

'Now, what's up, miss?'

I told them about him following me, then I showed them the note, and the box, said how it had been left there when the old man came in to buy his Italian poetry. The policeman picked up the box, the tissue still dangling out everywhere, and asked, 'What's in it?'

'You look, it's horrible, I don't know how he could have got them.'

He checked inside and smiled a little. 'Oh, look, ducks, it's just a practical joke, not very nice, but just plastic.' He picked up the hand and started waving it around. I shrank back, lifted my hands to hide the thing, and the woman cried out, 'What have you done to yourself, girl?' I started crying then, and she turned to the man.

'Phil, take a look around, will you, just to ease her mind, and I'll take her to the bathroom, help her clean up and dress that wound. What a rotten trick to play. Look, dearie, let's go to the bathroom.' She put her arm around me, and we walked upstairs.

I couldn't feel him any more, but this time, the thought made my stomach clench and I shivered a little. I put my hand out to reach for the light switch, and when I found it, I looked down the stairwell and saw that I'd left a great red smear along the wall.

'Don't worry, dear, it's just one of those superficial cuts that won't stop bleeding. We'll soon set you to rights. Then I'll help you clean up that wall and no one will be the wiser.'

We went into the toilet, and she put my hand under running

cold water while she rummaged about in the First Aid kit. She came over and wrenched the tap off, dried off my thumb, dolloped Savlon all over it and bandaged it up. She was a bit clumsy and abrupt, as though she didn't feel at ease with me. I sat down on the loo, and she leaned against the sink.

'Jokes like that make me feel nervous, I suppose because they're a bit malicious, aren't they? How long did you say you'd been bumping into this fellow? Since last August? And he's never done anything else like this? Are you sure it was the same chap?'

'Yeah, I know it was him. He once gave me a sheep's hoof, but I chucked it away real quick.'

'When was that?'

'Last November, I s'pose.' I didn't want to answer all her questions, it made me feel I was back at school, hauled up in front of the head.

'Why haven't you told anybody?'

'They'd think I was lying.'

'Do you lie often?'

'No, never. What're you getting at me for, I haven't done anything.'

'I'm sorry, I'm just trying to get the whole picture.'

I shrugged and stood up, wanting to get out of there, it was too small for both of us. I went along to the cupboard where I kept my coat and bag.

'I've got to get home, they'll get worried about me otherwise.'

'I think we'd better give you a lift. That'll be exciting, won't it, a ride in a police car?' As though I were some kid of seven. 'Hang on, and I'll just give that wall a wipe.' She came out of the bathroom with a cloth and rubbed at the smear, but it wouldn't shift.

'It'll take a lick of paint, I'm afraid. I'm sure your employer will understand. Everything all right downstairs, Phil?'

'Right as a rivet, Marj.' We left and the man locked the door behind us. He had the box and the note too.

The car wasn't as exciting as all that, just a two-way radio and the odd extra switch. PC Marj was dead proud of it though. She went on and on about it until she realised I wasn't listening, didn't care. She went all stiff and huffed. The fella,

Phil, had fallen asleep. She seemed glad to let me get out a couple of streets away from home when I asked. I didn't want Mum and Dad fussing at me, making me tell them why I was in a police car, persuading them I wasn't in trouble, like Johnny, my middle brother.

I walked along really slowly, feeling knackered. It was really quiet, all the houses lit up, the curtains drawn, everyone closed up in their homes, safe, tidy. Everything smelled fresh and new after the rain. A crowd of people came out, laughing and joking, all the girls dressed up, the chaps looking sort of casual, pretending to be cool. It made me fire up inside, why wasn't I going down to the pub or out to the disco? Because of some creepy sod with a sick sense of humour? I was steaming so much that I stopped dead and kicked a wall. My toe hurt, but I felt better inside, and I thought of what I must have looked like, kicking at that wall, my chin all stuck out and my fists clenched, that I laughed, and it felt like the first time in months. Then I knew what I had to do, I had to go and tell Old Glow-worm Eyes where he could put his plastic ears and sheeps' feet and his stupid mug, grinning at me all the time. I was going to tell him to shove off and grow up. I turned round and headed for the Common, and now I was walking fast, so fast I was practically running, but I wasn't breathless, I felt I could do anything, because I was going to show that bugger just where he got off.

When I reached the Common, I slowed down, just ambled down the path cutting through the middle, where I'd first bumped into him, I knew he'd turn up, sooner or later. I looked at my watch, it said 7:07:24 and I wondered how long it would take. I went up and down two more times, saw a couple of people out with their dogs, but nobody came near me. It was 7:19:43. The waiting put me on edge, and I suppose I started thinking of hearing that thump and then seeing his face mushed against the window, and the note, and I shivered, the anger was being worn down and away, the fear was coming back. My pace quickened up a bit, and as I reached the far end of the Common, near where I catch the bus, I thought that I'd better go on home now, maybe tell him off another time, or change jobs, find something a bit handier for home. Then I heard the footsteps behind me. I knew them. I knew that I'd never say anything to him, never be able to do anything, never escape.

I shoved my hands deep in the pocket of my tunic and felt the scalpel, and I thought, 'I have found a way to escape'. I grasped it very tight, and carried on, a little slower. The footsteps slowed down too, and I turned, lifting my arm and wiping the blade against the figure behind me. I moved in as he reeled back, and fell over, I bent down and stabbed and stabbed, mainly in the throat, that's where the animals got it, wasn't it, that was where he wanted to get them. He didn't fight back at all, he hadn't been expecting it. When I finished, I dropped the scalpel and curled up in a little ball, breathing deep to get my breath back. Then I looked up, and lost it all over again, because there he was, standing, watching with this little, happy smile on his face. I looked at the body and the eyes were wide open, glassy and very blue.

'I told you it was your turn next, love.'

In the distance I heard a siren as a breeze ruffled the trees at the edge of the Common.

I WONDER IF SHE'S
CHANGED

PAULA GOSLING

Paula Gosling was born in Detroit, but moved to England in 1964. She lives in Bath with her husband, John, her two children, Abigail and Emily, and three cats. She is currently Chairman of the Crime Writers' Association, and is very interested in promoting contacts between that organisation and readers of crime fiction.

Her novels include *Hoodwink*, *Monkey Puzzle* (which won The Gold Dagger as the Best Crime Novel of 1986) and *A Running Duck*, her first, upon which the film *Cobra* was (loosely) based. She says her hobby would be embroidery, if she could just find the time between writing, cooking, reading and looking after a husband, two daughters and three cats.

I Wonder if She's Changed appeared in *Women's Realm*, 1983

Liz was ironing when she heard it.

'. . . *on our Heartline today – a call for Liz Morrissey, sister of Peggy and daughter of Frank and Edna, last known in Darlington in 1974 . . .*'

She stood there, iron in hand, dressed in slip and blouse, late for work, with her blue skirt steaming gently on the board.

What on earth?

'. . . *if you're listening, Liz, Peggy would love to hear from you. Just ring us – or write to this address . .*'

The cheerful disc jockey's voice rose and fell through her confusion. How extraordinary to hear her name spoken out like that. Her maiden name, of course, and all the more penetrating as a result. She'd been Liz Morgan for nearly six

83

years now, but inside there still lived (and always would) little Lizzie Morrissey, small and meek and nearly forgotten.

She'd always been the lamb, gentle and agreeable. 'Biddable Bess' Dad had always called her, smiling as he spoke, and ruffling her hair. But she hadn't been very meek and mild when she'd decided to marry Don. And the more Mummy and Peg had railed at her, the more determined she'd become, with the deaf and dumb stubbornness of someone who, inside, is afraid everyone else just *might* be right.

But they'd backed her into a corner with their anger, until gathering the vestiges of her dignity around her, she'd fled with Don to South Africa. Wide-eyed, innocent, and incredibly stupid.

Don had seemed so heroic in England, bronzed and tall and strong. Once back in Johannesburg, however, he'd proved harsh and impatient. She'd tried to excuse it by blaming herself – as always – and tried to please him. In the end, of course, she realised she'd not been at fault at all. Only blind to what the country was and what it had made of him. Defeated, she'd divorced him and come home.

But not to Darlington and 'I told you so'. Oh, no. Still proud (or ashamed?), she'd built a new life and eventually a career. Now, promotion loomed – a real advancement in every way. She attacked the skirt once more, slamming the iron down, remembering her determination not to give in, not to admit defeat to anyone. In the one letter she'd gotten from Peg, she'd learned that Dad was dead (of a 'broken heart' Peg had snidely said) so what had there been to go back home *to*?

She swallowed down the lump in her throat. Something in you *always* wanted to go home. No matter how strong and independent you thought you were . . .

'. . . Peg says let bygones be bygones, Liz . . .' the disc jockey burbled on. Did she indeed? That didn't sound like Peg.

Liz lit a cigarette and blew smoke at the radio. I wonder if she's changed?, she thought. Must have taken brain surgery to do it if she has. Or perhaps just time.

Be fair.

Ten years' difference in age must always lead to problems between sisters, even if the older one *wasn't* 'conceited, nasty, spiteful, mean'. She grinned at herself, remembering how she used to crouch in the corner of their bedroom, chanting that very litany as Peg once again got her own way. But Peg was nearly forty, now. She *might* have mellowed.

'. . . *let's hear from you, Liz Morrissey* . . .'

She found she was reaching for the phone.

At some moment a last thread of reluctance had snapped within, and that hand was on its way to the past. She stared at it, wondering how it had become detached from her body, from her firm intentions, from her very heart and mind. Traitor hand, now it was dialling. Trying to go home again.

The disc jockey's voice had been replaced by a bouncy tune, and Liz had to reach over and turn down the volume to make herself heard. 'Hello? My name is Liz Morrissey – I'm calling on the Heartline . . .'

'Well, *I* think you're crazy.' Derek's voice was impatient with concern and affection. The noise of the pub swirled around their little table like tides around an island, isolating them. 'You didn't get on with her then, so why should you now? And raking up the past could be pretty unpleasant.'

'She sounded different. Really. She sounded as if she actually *cared*,' Liz said, poking an exploratory finger into his crisp packet. He snatched it out of calorie's way, picked up her hand and bit the end of her finger, gently. Liz smiled at him. It always surprised her when he did things like that, small tendernesses and silly surprises. you'd think someone who was so strong, so tough, really, wouldn't have that sweetness in him. But Derek did – and it usually undermined her. But not tonight. She was definitely going through with it, no matter what he said.

No matter what *anyone* said.

'She wanted to know if I was still married, and if I had any children. She's married, but she's never had any. And if I was happy, and . . . well . . . everything.'

Peg had also told her that Mother was dead. Liz had cried after putting down the phone, because Peg said Mother had only died a year or so ago. If Liz *had* gone back, things might have been different. She'd loved her mother, despite every-thing. And 'everything' included knowing that her mother's objections to her marriage had stemmed merely from concern for herself. Mother had wanted to keep dear little Liz under her thumb. But dear little Liz had slipped away like a melon seed, and run off to marry her older sister's boyfriend.

Oh Liz, she smiled to herself – you little poacher.

Nobody suspected for a minute, did they, until it was too late? Not even *you*, come to that. You simply couldn't *believe* someone like Don would prefer mousey little Liz to sophisticated Peg. When he swept you off your feet, it wasn't love you felt, it was amazement.

Of *course* she wanted to know everything,' Derek was saying. 'I hope, for your own sake, that you didn't . . .'

'I have to do it, Derek,' Liz said. She stood up abruptly, not wanting him to get through the careful, nervous defences she'd built up. 'I can't go on wondering why – I have to *know*.'

'Then let me come with you,' he said for the hundredth time.

She wavered momentarily. 'No, I can't. She asked if I'd like to bring someone, and I said I'd be coming alone. I can't just suddenly turn up with an extra mouth to feed.' She grinned at him. 'Especially *your* mouth, you bottomless pit.'

'I have to keep up my strength to look after you,' he told her, not smiling at all, except with his eyes. 'Come on then – I'll drive you over.'

The big mock-Georgian house on the suburban street was a long way from the council terrace on the wrong side of Darlington, Liz thought, as she walked up the path next to the sweep of gravelled drive. Beyond the thick hedge that hid the garden from the street, she heard the roar of Derek's Rover pulling away.

The speed with which the glossy front door opened told her Peg had been waiting for her arrival, perhaps had even watched her coming up the drive.

'Liz . . . *darling* . . .'

Peg has put on weight, Liz thought, as she was swept into a hug – practically the first hug she'd ever had from her older sister. Over Peg's shoulder she could see the black and white tiles of the hallway, the antiques and paintings, the carpeted curve of the stairway. It's all this that's changed her, she thought. Having all this.

'Hello, Peg.' They stared at one another for a moment, then

Peggy smiled. 'Come and meet Robert. There's so much to catch up on, love. So many years.'

In the flawlessly decorated lounge, Robert Cornwall got to his feet and held out a hand to her. Tall, attractive, well-dressed in cashmere cardigan and slacks over a silk shirt, Robert Cornwall was apparently the consolation prize that Peg had found after losing Dashing Don to her younger sister. Robert must have provided a great deal of consolation indeed, Liz thought.

'Well, well – Peg said you'd be lovely, Liz, and you are. Welcome home,' Robert said, warmly.

'Yes, love, welcome home,' Peg echoed, beaming at her. 'And I hope you *will* consider this home from now on. After all, we're all we've got, now.'

'Well –' Liz considered mentioning Derek, then thought it best left for later. 'Blood is thicker than water, I suppose,' she said, and wondered where in the name of all that's holy she'd found the gall to utter *that* one. But Peg nodded, and smiled, and she realised that the cliché had only confirmed what Peg remembered of her younger sister. Awkward, unimaginative, meek and shy. Biddable Bess has come home, Peg's eyes said.

Robert bustled about, getting drinks from behind the doors of an antique tall-boy, selecting from a formidable array of bottles. Nothing in poor taste, of course, like a bar or a tray of drinks. Oh no, not here. Everything discreet, hidden away.

'There we are,' Robert said, handing Liz her gin and tonic. 'Here's to coming home.' They all raised their glasses, drank dutifully, and then sat waiting for someone to make everything easier. Robert cleared his throat.

'Well. Peg said you're working as a civil servant now, is that right?'

'Yes.'

'Not in the Tax Office, I hope,' Robert said, with a jolly laugh.

'No – you're quite safe from me,' Liz offered, brightly. 'Tax-wise, that is. I don't know what *else* you've been up to, of course.' She'd meant it as a joke. After a moment, they both decided to take it as one, and offered small smiles in return.

'Robert's in Property,' Peggy said, giving sufficient emphasis to the word to imply that he owned half of Mayfair.

'How fascinating,' Liz said, and almost meant it. She turned to face Peg. 'Tell me about Mother. Did she – '

'It was very quick,' Peg said, briskly. 'She didn't suffer at all. Heart attack.'

'Oh.' It hadn't been what she'd intended to ask, but it sufficed.

'It really was a shame about – all the difficulty,' Robert commented, putting his drink carefully into the coaster waiting on the little table beside him and taking out a thin cigar. 'I find it very sad that families can lose touch like that, over some small disagreement, everyone too proud to say they're wrong – '

'Well, I *was* wrong,' Liz admitted. 'Don was very persuasive, and I was so young and inexperienced . . . '

'Oh, he was silver-tongued, all right,' Peg agreed, quickly. 'I never *really* trusted him, myself.'

Liz looked at her in surprise, remembering the vicious hiss of her voice on that long-ago night. 'I'll always hate you for this. I'll never forget . . . '

'Of course, we weren't certain whether you'd actually come back to England,' Robert went on. 'But I often hear that Heartline thing on the car radio as I'm moving about, and I suggested to Peg that it might be worth a try. She'd never heard of it, of course. Strictly Radio Three, aren't you, love?'

'Can't stand all that chat and noise they call music,' Peg said, lightly. Liz, looking at her more closely, saw that despite her tone there was tension in her plump face, especially around the mouth. Her eyes kept darting at Liz and then away, taking her in sips, like a furtive alcoholic. Peg smoothed her dress over her knees and picked up a bit of fluff to roll between her well manicured fingertips. 'Of course, I didn't much like the idea of *broadcasting* our differences, so to speak, but since I used our maiden name I didn't suppose it would make any difference. Nobody would connect it to *us*, after all.' She looked at her sister and smiled. 'I suppose when you heard it you were very surprised?'

'Well, of course.'

'We couldn't even be certain you listened to *that* station,' Peg went on, as if anyone *would*, given the choice. 'Of course, a friend of yours might have heard it and told you, there was always that chance. Were your friends surprised? When you told them?'

Liz flushed. 'No. That is . . .'

Robert gave a sudden bark of laughter. 'You haven't told them, have you? Quite right, too. Had to see if we were acceptable or not, yes? Just what I would have done, myself, in your place. A private thing. Delicate. We *might* have been the world's worst, after all.' He laughed again, confident that she could see the situation was actually the exact opposite.

'So might I,' Liz said, defensively.

Peg leaned over and patted her hand. 'Oh, no – I knew you'd be just the same, love. Sweet and shy, as always. I hope you weren't too hurt by your marriage breaking up. I *knew* he'd be bad for you. You were always so sensitive.'

Crybaby, you used to call me, Liz thought, looking into the bright blue eyes and the slightly wavered line of shadow on the lids above them. Peg was beautifully made up and turned out, but here and there, her nervousness showed. Had she really been worried about me and what I might be like? Liz found that difficult to believe. Not Peg. Peg had never worried about what other people might be like. Peg, after all, was Peg, and they'd have to accept that. Peg got her way. Peg had *always* got her way.

As they went on talking, in between the awkward silences, Liz realised that this wasn't going to work. Peg simply had wanted her to come and bear witness to the fact that, after all, Peg was the winner and Liz the loser. The differences were still there, and always would be. She couldn't imagine herself and Derek coming here, nor imagine Peg and Robert coming to them. She just *couldn't*. Nothing in common, nothing to say to one another. Indeed, when Robert rather expansively began to hold forth on the current economic situation, she imagined Derek's comments and nearly laughed aloud. Derek was so damned irreverent.

'Is Mother buried in Darlington?'

They stared at her, glasses suspended. 'Why, yes,' Peg said, after a moment. 'Beside Daddy, in that cemetery on the hill above the river. With the Whitbys.' Her tone was complacent as she settled down from Liz's surprise question.

The Whitbys. Liz made a small grimace. Mother had always

flaunted the Whitbys, made Dad constantly aware of how lucky he'd been to catch one. And those Sunday visits to that mausoleum of a house where the last of them lived, two maiden aunts and an uncle. Unmarried and unlovely, their dark halls and dark lives were filled with imagined slights, despair, plots, and petty spite. They only visited them because of the 'expectations', of course. Uncle Haven was supposed to have piled up millions. 'Are they all dead, then?' Liz asked.

'All dead,' Peg said, with a brittle, bitter laugh. 'And it was all *sham*, every bit of it. They were as poor as church mice, the lot of them. No wonder they never went out, and dressed in those old clothes. They were pretending. Robert even had to pay the funeral expenses for Uncle Haven in the end, can you imagine it?'

'Least I could do,' Robert boomed. 'I hold family to be very important, as I told Peg when I urged her to try that radio thing to find you. Families. When you come down to it, what else is there you can count on?'

A great deal, Liz thought – but maybe you don't know that. 'I suppose I ought to go up there, sometime. To her grave, I mean. To say goodbye.'

'Sounds morbid to me,' Peg sniffed. 'And not at *all* necessary.'

'Even so, I think I will,' Liz said, firmly. 'I'll take a couple of days off next week and go. Why don't you come with me, Peg?'

'Oh. Oh, no – I couldn't do that,' Peg said, glancing at her husband. 'I mean, I have several committee meetings and – '

'Peg keeps busy,' Robert put in, smoothly. 'Peg *likes* to keep busy, don't you, love? Charities, and so on. I say, your glass is empty, Liz. Let me get you a refill.'

Twenty minutes later, Peg looked at her sister slumped in the corner of the sofa. 'I thought it would never work. One aspirin used to put her right to sleep as a kid.'

'People change,' Robert observed.

'Not Liz, she's the same mealy-mouthed little cow she always was. "Oh, it's so nice to have a family again",' Peg mimicked, cruelly. 'But not for long, dear sister. Not for long.'

'Why do you hate her so?' Robert asked, taking off the soft

cardigan he'd been wearing. He folded it carefully and put it over the arm of the chair.

'No concern of yours,' Peg snapped. 'Just get on with it. They'll be home, soon, and I have to clear up.' She rubbed frantically at a damp place on the edge of the sofa cushion where Liz's glass had fallen from her limp fingers. 'My God, if the Cornwalls walked in now – '

It was an unprepossessing stretch of canal, running between the factories and the reservoir. Overhead, the glow of the city turned the low clouds to a pale orange that reflected dully from the oily surface of the dark water. A few feet from the edge a black plastic bag drifted, obscenely bloated with someone's garden refuse. Or worse.

Robert laid his burden down thankfully, and took out his handkerchief to wipe his face. Liz was a small girl, but solid, and heavier than he'd thought she'd be. Well, one did what one had to do, especially when the prize was so great. Unlike Peg, however, *he* regretted it.

Kneeling down on the cinders of the path that ran along the canalside, he removed Liz's shoes. He read they always remove their shoes. Then he took the note out of his jacket pocket. The last page of a letter from South Africa, undated, and all in Liz's own handwriting. Never answered, of course – but kept. Clever Peg. Too bad she couldn't hold on to money or her tongue as easily as she held on to things like this letter, he thought. Or hate.

And the letter was perfect. '. . . I'm sorry to have caused you so much pain . . . please try to forgive me . . . Liz.'

He wondered who the 'you' would be presumed to be. Boss? Boyfriend? But of course, they'd be surprised, whoever it was. People were *always* surprised by suicides. A reason was always looked for, and grasped at, however remote. 'Why, I had no idea he (she) was so unhappy. She (he) always seemed so normal.'

How else could they live with the guilt of possibly having neglected or misunderstood a loved one or friend? She (he) was overworked (or bored), remorseful (or a victim of circumstances), repressed (or promiscuous), ill (or neurotic), worried (or strangely carefree), etc. (or etc.).

Oh, yes.

He removed her coat, put the note inside, and folded it on top of her shoes. Looking around, he shivered. Overhead the massive electricity pylons loomed in the night like giant watchmen, humming eerily to themselves. Below them the factory yards were still. Rusted junk back here, mostly, not worth guarding. A breeze strummed the high-tension wires, and the dark water sucked at the bank of the canal.

He picked her up and carried her to the water's edge. Her breathing was heavy and slow. There wouldn't be a mark on her, of course. And the combination of gin and sleeping pills in her stomach wasn't enough to kill her. Lots of suicides needed Dutch courage.

She'd said she'd told no one about her reunion with Peg. But even if she had, the name and address would prove to be no help. Mr and Mrs Cornwall would know nothing about it. How about the couple who work for you? the police might ask (if they bothered to pursue the matter at all). And the Cornwalls would say Good Heavens, no, Robert and Margaret Ashby are *perfect* servants.

His mouth twisted. They *had* been perfect servants, too. Smiling and nodding and watching the Cornwalls wearing expensive clothes, going on expensive holidays, and entertaining expensive friends – and then niggling with Peg over their wages and the household expenses. They'd put up with it, they'd had to put up with it, because Peg's mother had taken against Robert over that matter of the cheque. The old bitch.

He set his jaw, trying to build up his anger sufficiently to get this dreadful business over with. My God, if Liz *had* gone up to Darlington, she would have discovered her mother still alive in the nursing home. She would have heard the whole story (slanted, of course) about that cheque. She would have found out about Uncle Haven's millions sitting in the bank, too. Then the fat would have been in the fire. Time had been short, once they learned about the old lady's cancer. If she'd been reconciled with Liz she might have changed her will yet again. After the fuss about the forged cheque, it had taken all Peg's persuasive powers to keep the old arrangement in force – equal shares between the two girls was as far as Mother Morrissey would go. The old bag had a grudging respect for tradition and felt even an estranged daughter should be remembered. He would have been happy with half a million, himself, but Peg wanted it all. He didn't know what the trouble had been between the sisters, but apparently it was sufficient to make murder preferable to sharing.

He put Liz's legs over the side.

The people at the radio station had been *so* nice about putting lonely Miss Morrissey in touch with her long-lost sister. They'd passed Liz's phone number over to Peg, and their work was done. It was up to Peg whether she called her sister or not, but they *hoped* she would. Sentiment made an excellent anaesthetic for suspicion. How nice for them to feel they'd done a good deed in a naughty world. Robert smiled in the dark. And how nice for us.

He slid Liz's body closer to the edge.

In a few days they'd give in their notice to the Cornwalls and then 'disappear'. They would return to Darlington and hold the old lady's hand until she went. It was just a matter of waiting. And then being very surprised when a search by the solicitors revealed that the long-lost sister had committed suicide. How tragic.

He braced himself and started to ease Liz's weight over the edge. He'd hold her under to make certain. If she sank down into the mud it might be days before –

Someone huge and strong and very angry took hold of his arms, and Liz slipped away into the black water. Gaping, he saw her thrash about and grab for the side. She was awake! A policeman was helping her out! Another one was bellowing at him about attempted murder and arrest!

Robert was stunned by the instant transition from dark silence to noise and flashlights and fury. 'But – I was trying to stop her – there must be some mistake – ' he blustered.

Liz was standing up now, glaring at him. 'The only mistake was *mine*,' she said, her teeth chattering. 'I thought you'd wait a few days before trying to kill me.'

'*I* didn't,' Derek muttered, thrusting Robert into the arms of one of the uniformed officers he'd summoned on his car radio. 'That's why I came back and hung around, watching. A good thing you signalled me behind his back when he carried you out, or I'd have moved in then. As it is – '

'But it wasn't my idea, she told me . . . ,' Robert whined.

Liz regarded him with disgust. How like Peg to pick this pathetic specimen, all surface and no substance, easy to keep in line. The edgy way he'd watched her when she sipped her drink had warned her it might be drugged. She'd had to take a bit for appearance, but managed to dribble the rest away between the sofa cushions. If she'd been wrong, the only result would have been a small stain. But she'd been right. Anger was rapidly clearing her head.

'Did you really think I'd believe her?' she demanded. 'Did she *really* think I'd come along, meek as a lamb, grateful for crumbs from my wealthy sister? I *hoped* she'd changed, but I knew Peg, knew her of old. There was no generosity in her, and no forgiveness, either. If she wanted to get in touch with me now, after all these years, there had to be a reason – and probably not a good reason, either. Peg hasn't changed, but *I have*! So I checked up, in Darlington and down here, because checking up on things is part of my job. *You* should have checked on *me* before you tried your little game.'

As they took him away, she swayed and staggered slightly. Derek went to her, and grinned down at her filthy clothes. Canal water dripped from the hem of her skirt, and smears of oil and muddy weed were all over her stockings. One shoe was lost for ever.

'Time you got into some dry things, Sgt Morgan. I know you're being promoted to CID next week, but don't you think this is carrying the idea of plain clothes just a little too far?'

THE SMALL MAN'S REVENGE

T. N. TRAN

T. N. Tran studied law before working in advertising, computers, and running her own knitwear boutique under her own label. She is keenly interested in photography, travel, aromatherapy, polarity – and murder.

The small man stood just inside the door. He hadn't moved. Surprise mingled with disappointment pinched his face.

'Oh,' he said, 'I hadn't expected a . . . a woman.'

I indicated a chair in front of my desk.

'Come in, please. Take a seat.'

He moved across the small room and sat down as though the chair might be booby-trapped. He looked around the dingy little office, the dusty box files, the second-hand filing cabinet, the various odds and ends. His gaze returned to me and to the cluttered desk I was sitting at. It was cluttered for a very good reason: I had cluttered it. I moved an empty whisky bottle slightly, giving it a more rakish position in relation to the enormous ashtray, the folded copy of the racing paper, the usual odds and ends I thought a client might reasonably expect to see on a private eye's desk: a private eye who was not beyond the financial reach of just such a man as the little fellow sitting opposite me now. The emotional reach, too . . . . People are too easily overawed, I find, particularly in England. They clam up when confronted with any ostentation of wealth or power. It's the Them and Us syndrome. I know it well. I was always an Us.

I leaned back in my wooden swivel chair and considered whether to rest an ankle on the edge of the desk. I decided, no. There are some things . . . .

'Is this all of your office?'

The little man's eyes were rolling around in his head as he surveyed his surroundings.

'That's correct.'

His eyes homed in on my desk top.

'And the whisky . . . ?'

'Mine as well. Unfortunately you got here a little late. I'm afraid I haven't a drop left to offer you.'

'Oh, that's quite all right. I don't drink. Not really.'

'Just a little quart occasionally, huh?'

He missed the attempt at humour.

'I don't drink milk,' he said. 'I don't touch dairy products.'

'Each to his own, Mr . . . uh?'

'Snipcott. Arthur Snipcott.'

'How do you do, Mr Snipcott.' I smiled at him. 'Now, what can I do . . .?'

I stopped. Mr Snipcott was staring at the ashtray. The ashtray was loaded with fat, brown, rather gruesome cigar butts.

'Do you?' he began hesitantly. 'Do you smoke those things?'

'Just what you see . . . .'

'Ah . . . .'

He looked quite astonished.

'It's strange . . .' he went on.

'What's that?'

'They don't appear to . . . to pong.'

To pong. The words somehow expressed the man. While he'd been doing his Al Jolson act, rolling his eyes around the room, my office, I'd been sizing him up as private eyes do when confronted with another person who is going to figure in any way prominently in the events that are to follow. Mr Snipcott, I decided, was one of nature's timid souls. He had a small moustache that drooped, like everything else about Mr Snipcott: eyes, mouth, shoulders. The quintessential little man who wouldn't say boo to a goose. I could not, of course, reveal to him that the cigar butts had been carefully gathered and deodorised with air freshener.

'I thought, you see . . . I thought the sign . . .'

The shingle downstairs was painted gilt on brown.

ACME DETECTIVE AGENCY
3rd Floor

Then, under that:

Proprietor: Jay Acme

'You thought the Jay sounded like a man, right?'

'Exactly. In fact . . .'

'Yes?'

'I thought it sounded rather . . . *transatlantic*, to be honest.'

'Well, you're not too far out there, Mr Snipcott. I have a mixed background. Scots. Irish. American. Canadian. Cherokee. You name it. Not, unfortunately,' I said, with deference to my present company and our surroundings, 'not a drop of English.'

Mr Snipcott leaned forward in his hard chair. His eyes widened.

'It's a very confidential matter, you see . . . I wouldn't like it to . . . you know . . .'

I nodded my head slowly. 'Get around.'

'Yes, yes. Exactly.' Mr Snipcott said.

I gave him my reassuring professional smile.

'Then you have come to the right place, Mr Snipcott. The motto of the Acme Detective Agency is simple: Discretion is the Better Part of Valour. Whatever is said within these four walls remains here. Your secrets are our secrets.' Quickly I flipped open the first page of my notebook and clicked my pen ready. 'Now what exactly seems to be the problem, Mr Snipcott . . . ?'

'It's the brown envelopes,' Mr Snipcott said. 'They've been coming for over a month now. When I get home from work they're lying there, on the mat, inside the door, waiting . . . . They're unmarked, of course. But that doesn't mean anything, does it . . . ? I mean, everybody knows what comes in brown envelopes, don't they?'

I thought of the various things that come in brown envelopes. Rates bills, electricity bills, gas bills, water bills . . . . Not, of course, *unmarked* brown envelopes . . . .

'Tell me, Mr Snipcott. What exactly does come in these brown envelopes?'

'Oh, very nasty magazines . . . I can't see why anybody would want to publish such things.'

'People publish things other people want to buy.'

'Then they must be very sick people, that's all I can say.'

'What kind of magazines are we talking about exactly, Mr Snipcott?'

Mr Snipcott lowered his voice as though afraid somebody might overhear. 'They've got pictures. Of young people. Very young people. Children, really.'

'Pornographic pictures, you mean?'

'Oh. Very.'

'I see.'

I tapped my fingertips on the empty whisky bottle for a while.

'You may speak frankly within these four walls, Mr Snipcott. Have you ever subscribed to such magazines?'

'Oh, no.'

'Or other magazines, of a roughly similar nature, let's say.'

'Never. Well . . .'

'Yes?'

'Some years ago, I was going through a difficult period at the time, at work. I work for a firm of stockbrokers, you see . . . and the pressure was on . . . . The Big Bang, as they called it, was coming up . . . . A very difficult period . . . .'

'You're a stockbroker?'

If I sounded surprised, I was.

'Oh, no. That's too grand for my job. I'm really just a clerk. A glorified clerk really. Well, perhaps not glorified even.'

'Go on, Mr Snipcott.'

'At that time . . . I did sometimes go over to the West End of an evening . . . have dinner and a glass of wine . . . a little Italian place called San Michele. Afterwards, well, there are these shops over there, in Soho. I don't know if you know the kind of shop. They sell magazines. Picture magazines.'

He looked at me appealingly, willing me to comprehend without any further explanation on his part.

'Girlie magazines, you mean?'

He nodded sheepishly.

'Big girls, I take it.'

'Oh, absolutely. I give you my word. Very big girls indeed, some of them.'

'Never any other magazines . . . featuring children?'

'Definitely not. I can't imagine why anyone would want such things.'

'What do you mean?'

'I mean I can't stand children. Nasty little creatures. Why anyone would want . . . '

'OK,' I said. 'I get the picture. Tell me, Mr Snipcott. Did you subscribe to any of these magazines you mentioned? Give your name and address? Join a club? Anything like that?'

'Oh, no. I wouldn't ever have done that.'

'So you were just an anonymous customer browsing after a hard day's work . . . '

'Exactly . . .'

'Then this is strange . . .'

He seemed relieved to find me sympathetic. 'I was hoping you would be willing to help me.'

'I didn't say that. I'd need a little more information first. Then if I can be of any help . . . . Of course,' I added sternly, 'my fees are not the lowest in the business.'

'Oh, I shouldn't worry about that.'

'Well, then . . . .' I flicked to a fresh page. 'Let us commence. Your full name, Mr Snipcott . . . .'

Arthur Henry Snipcott, fifty-two, was a bachelor. Employed by Chivers and Bull, a prominent City stockbrokers. Twenty-seven years with the same firm. His private residence was a flat in Bayswater. He lived alone. He had never married and his nearest living relative was a second cousin somewhere in New Zealand. He had no enemies, apparently no friends. His world was circumscribed by the Central Line which daily carried him from Queensway Tube station to St Paul's station. He bought a weekly ticket and used the ticket occasionally on a Saturday to visit the West End where he might see a movie in one of the big cinemas. Apart from that his sole interest seemed to be reading political biographies.

'Can you think of anyone who might have sent these magazines to you? Somebody who thought you might be interested, perhaps . . . . Or,' I went on quickly, 'somebody with a grudge. Somebody who wanted to cause you trouble?'

For the magazines were certainly illegal. A few years back an organisation that published such magazines was closed down and the organisers put in jail. Mr Snipcott could possibly join them there if the police got word of his magazine collection.

'No,' Mr Snipcott said, a strained look on his face. 'I can think of no one.'

'Where are the magazines now?'

'In my flat.'

'I think you should get them out of there as soon as possible. Bring them here. I'll put them under lock and key.'

'You think the police might . . . might raid me?'

He sounded for a moment like a strip-club owner operating on the edge of the law.

'Let's assume somebody is trying to set you up. We don't know who. We don't know why. Not yet . . . . In the meantime, we take no chances.'

'It's my lunch hour. I'll go now.'

'Good,' I said, 'we can't be too careful.'

Mr Snipcott took fifty minutes to return with his bundle of brown envelopes. In that time I made a few phone calls. Before I poured my redundancy money into setting up the Acme Detective Agency I had been a legal secretary. It's amazing what you can pick up as a legal secretary, not only information, but useful contacts. I called Larry Wiles, a legal clerk in King's Bench Walk. He worked for a firm of barristers who specialise in financial cases. He knew all about Mr Snipcott's employer.

'The grapevine has it that you know who (meaning Chivers and Bull) are among companies being investigated or about to be investigated for stock rigging, insider trading and other assorted gentlemen's games. Why, what's the interest?'

'General,' I said.

'I'm sure.'

The legal profession is packed to the rafters with doubting Thomases.

'What's the procedure with these investigations, Larry?'

'What do you mean exactly?'

'How do they go about it?'

'They go into the company concerned. They go through the records. They cross-question people involved.'

'Sounds familiar,' I said. 'You mean they ask the big boys if they've been naughty and they say no, we haven't, and they say, okay, that's all right then, and everybody goes round the corner to the club and gets sloshed in celebration.'

'There is that,' Larry said. 'But they aren't allowed to leave it at that any more. Too much bad publicity. Harming England's good name abroad and all that hogwash. No, they pursue it right down the line . . . even down to lowly little bods like you and me.'

'Who, you lowly, Larry?' I said. 'Earning more than the top barristers in your chambers, nice big percentages coming your way from all over the shop?'

'I love you when you're being cynical, Jay. I really do.'

We promised one another lunch some time soon and hung up. Mr Snipcott stood in the doorway with his bundle.

'That was quick.'

'I ran part of the way.'

'Give them here then.'

He sat down in his chair again and breathed heavily while I took the bundle of brown envelopes and tucked them at the back of one of the big file drawers, behind a portable car Hoover, which I use around the office, and a pile of old phone directories which had been left behind by a previous tenant.

'Tell me, Mr Snipcott, who is your immediate boss at Chivers and Bull?'

'Why, Mr Newby.'

'How do you get on with him?'

'Oh, er, all right, I suppose.'

I recognised the sounds.

'Is he new to the Company?'

'He is, as a matter of fact. They brought him in especially . . . . He's very experienced.'

'What's your function exactly, in relation to Mr Newby?'

'Well, he makes the transactions, does the big deals. I do the paperwork. A glorified pen-pusher. That's what I am, really. Not really . . . .'

'Glorified, even. I know. In other words, you know everything that's going through the Company.'

'In our sector. In our sector. We're all in sectors.'

'Anything dodgy going through at times?'

A curious stillness came over Mr Snipcott's features. It was as if some blood had been drained from him. He went very still and pale. And proper.

'I am afraid I do not know quite what you are referring to, Mrs Acme.'

'Miss. Miss Acme.'

'I beg your pardon. Miss Acme. 'I'm afraid . . . '

'One hears rumours,' I cut in. 'Insider trading. Stock rigging. That sort of thing.'

From the look on Mr Snipcott's face I knew I had jammed both feet right into the holy of holies. He seemed to draw himself up in the chair, like a Plasticine man.

'I have never done a dishonest thing in my life, Miss Acme. I resent the suggestion.'

'Hold on,' I said. 'Nobody was accusing you of anything. But maybe some others, with gold fever in their blood, maybe they . . .'

'I have said it before and I shall say it again.' Mr Snipcott said, and I could see his study of politicians hadn't gone to waste. It's their favourite phrase. That and 'I promise you that if elected . . .'

'I never reveal the Company's business to anyone. Unless . . .'

I waited. 'Unless what, Mr Snipcott?'

'I shouldn't have said that.'

'But you did. What did you mean?'

He was silent.

'Unless it's to the properly constituted authorities? Is that what you said, Mr Snipcott?'

Then a new thought hit me.

'Who did you say this to, Mr Snipcott? Mr Newby?'

'I shall say no more.' He got to his feet. 'I'm afraid this has been a mistake, my coming here. I think I had better be getting back . . . .'

And with that Mr Snipcott turned and hurried out of the office. It was a moment before I remembered the pile of brown envelopes in the filing cabinet. When I reached the landing, though, he was already out of the building. I went back into the office and got out the envelopes and looked at them.

Each of them had been typed. On an electric machine, using a carbon ribbon. The impression was sharp as a needle. Whoever had done the typing, though, hadn't much of a touch. Letters were jammed together as when an unfamiliar hand pecks at the keyboard. Not a professional typist.

I had a mind to let Mr Snipcott go hang. I mean, it doesn't do much for a private detective's reputation to go chasing after clients. Chasing after baddies, yes. After clients, no. At least not overtly. I stuffed the brown envelopes with their incriminating contents back into the filing cabinet and locked it. For the rest of that day and the next I busied myself in a very un-detective-like pursuit, checking credit applications against voters' registers. Boring work, but it helps pay the rent.

I was getting on to the Tube at Chancery Lane on the second evening when I saw the front page of somebody else's evening paper. There was a picture of Mr Snipcott. And the headline: POLICE SEEK TUBE BROLLY KILLER.

I jumped off the train and went upstairs and bought a copy of the paper. I stood there reading the story on the front page, impervious to the jostling crowd all around me. Mr Snipcott, it appeared, had been murdered.

Next morning all the tabloids carried a photograph of an eyewitness. Miss Rachel Smail, twenty-six, secretary in an insurance company, had been standing along the platform from Mr Snipcott when the murder took place.

'I was no more than twenty feet away. Of course there were plenty of other people waiting for the train on the platform. But I clearly saw this umbrella. It was a gentleman's brolly, neatly rolled up. It went out, straight like, just as the train came down the tunnel. It seemed to stab this little man in the back and then somebody screamed. But it was too late. The train ran right over him. It was horrible, horrible . . . .'

Miss Smail lived in Greenford, Middlesex, and after a phone call I went to see her. She was taking a few days off work to recover, she explained. She seemed remarkably chipper, however, and it took me a good five minutes to assure her that

I had no intention of crossing her palm with silver. Some of the tabloids had already coughed up, it appeared, and this had apparently whetted her appetite.

'Did you see the man with the brolly?'

'I couldn't get a look at him. There were so many people all around.'

'Funny nobody else saw it happen.'

'What's funny about it? You know people on the Tube. Staring straight ahead. Like a row of convicts. Death Row I call 'em.' She put a hand over her mouth and giggled behind it. 'Oh, I shouldn't have said that. I feel bad . . . .'

'You'll get over it, I'm sure,' I said. 'What made you look along the platform, Miss Smail?'

'I don't know. I like to watch people. They're funny. Oh, I remember. It was the little bloke. The bloke that got murdered. He was looking around over his shoulder all the time. One of them freaky middle-aged types. You know them. The Tube's full of them. There's one bloke talks to himself all the time and salutes like he was in the army or something. Another keeps a hankie up his sleeve and dusts the seat before he sits down. This one was jumping about like a chicken on a griddle. I never saw anybody look as scared. Scared of his own shadow.'

'Did he see the man with the brolly behind him?'

'*I* don't know.'

She stopped and appeared lost in thought.

'What is it?'

'I've just remembered something. Isn't that a caution! Forgot all about it till you started me thinking.'

'Remembered what, Miss Smail?'

'Oh, call me Rachel. All the photographers do. It was a thing on his wrist. At least I think it was *his* wrist.'

'The dead man's?'

'No, silly. Sorr-ee. I mean the bloke with the brolly. He had a thing on his wrist. I saw it kind of gleam when he stretched his arm. It caught the light.'

'What, a bracelet?'

'Yeah. No. One of them things people wear. Supposed to cure your aches and pains or something. Miracle something or other.'

'A copper bracelet . . . is that what you mean?'

'Yeah. I think so. I remember thinking it looked a bit phoney on a bloke, a bracelet. Then I thought, no, you're wrong, it's for his aches and pains . . . . Here,' she leaned forward from the sofa. 'What do you think? You think it's valuable, that? Think it's worth much?'

'I think you can buy them for eight or nine quid. You see them advertised in the papers sometimes.'

'No, not the bracelet, stupid!' She giggled uproariously again. 'Sorr-ee. I mean the *information* . . . . Here. I shouldn't have given that out to you. It's got to be worth something.'

I took out my Filofax and extracted a fiver.

'Here!' Miss Smail said, snatching it from my hand. 'Is that all it's worth?'

'What do you think it's worth?'

She looked puzzled. 'I dunno . . .'

I added a second fiver to the first. 'There, how's that? Under the counter. No tax . . .'

Miss Smail squirmed in her mother's sofa. 'Ee, that's better . . . . Gosh, I only wish . . .' She stopped and giggled again. 'Oh, my, that is naughty of me, thinking like that. Sorr-ee!'

Mr Snipcott's office was a cubbyhole, the walls lined with shelves on which file boxes, labelled cryptically, provided the sole adornment.

'Call me if you want anything,' the young lady called Miss Peabody said. 'I'm just next door.'

'Were you his secretary?' I asked. I sniffed into my crumpled lace handkerchief.

'I'm afraid not. Mr Snipcott didn't have a secretary of his own. He used the pool. But most of the time he didn't need typing.'

'And what do you do, Miss?' I enquired meekly.

'I'm Mr Newby's secretary.'

'Oh, yes. I think my poor departed brother mentioned the name. He was Arthur's boss, wasn't he?'

'That's right.' She cocked her head at the sound of a buzzer. 'That's him now. I'm sorry but I must run. Do call if you need any help.'

I sniffled again into the tiny handkerchief. 'You're so kind, my dear, so kind . . . '

She tiptapped quickly along the corridor in her impossibly high heels and I stopped sniffling, shoved the lace handkerchief into my pocket, straightened my shoulders and took a look around the windowless broom closet that had been Mr Snipcott's office.

Now that I was in the office, I didn't know what I was looking for exactly. I went through the drawers. There were a few personal odds and ends. I put them in the plastic shopping bag I'd brought with me. I was about to turn my attention to the box files lining the wall when a very posh voice, very loud, very confident and very close by, made me jump round.

'They tell me you're Mr Snipcott's sister.'

'Was,' I said. 'I mean . . . '

'I get your meaning. How do you do, I'm Jonathan Newby.'

'Oh, indeed, indeed. Arthur often spoke very highly of you.'

He seemed amused at this. 'How kind of him,' he drawled.

'I was just gathering up his few personal belongings.' I showed him the contents of the plastic shopping bag. 'Palgrave's *Golden Treasury* . . . *A Life of Lloyd George* . . . two packets of Fox's Glacier Mints . . . one half eaten . . .'

Mr Jonathan Newby dismissed the rest of the inventory with a magnanimous wave of his hand. He strolled towards the facing wall, which was no more than four feet away, then swung round and returned. With his hands clasped behind his back, he looked like a penguin on patrol. 'Tell me, did your brother ever discuss his work with you, at home, I mean, you know . . . ?'

I looked astonished at the notion. 'Oh, my goodness me, no. Arthur was the height of discretion . . . . I used to say sometimes he was like a priest . . . with his vow of secrecy . . . you know, *sub rosa* and all that. Not,' I added, 'that it would have meant a thing to me anyway . . . . He was the one with a head for figures in our family.' I offered him the evidence of the grocery bag again. 'Managing my shopping list is more than enough for me.'

'I see,' Mr Jonathan Newby said. Then like a commanding officer about to dismiss his troops, he barked, 'Good. Good. Carry on then.'

I heard his military step dwindle down the long corridor and silence returned. It was amazing how silent the office was. All those computers and things can be very quiet at times. I tugged my handkerchief out of my pocket in readiness and went next door. Mr Newby's secretary wasn't there. I looked down the corridor. In the far distance I could see two small heads bent together over a desk. Apart from that I seemed to have the place to myself suddenly. I went over to the big electric typewriter . . . .

Mr Newby had a large office, with a fine view out over the crowded City of London. His desk was enormous and very modern and when I slipped behind it the soft leather of his big swivel chair sighed gently. There were three drawers on each side of his desk and I found what I was looking for in the bottom one of the right-hand side. I quickly folded it and stuffed it into my pocket. I was about to close the drawer when something caught my eye. There, half-hidden, lay a copper rheumatism bracelet.

'Thank you, my dear, I'll be running along now. You've been very kind.'
   Mr Newby's secretary had returned to her office.
   'You're finished then?'
   'Oh, yes. Just these few things . . .'
   'Can you find your way back to the lift all right?'
   'Yes, don't you worry about me. Goodbye.'
   'Goodbye,' the girl said. 'And I'm so sorry . . . .'

It was a new office block that housed Chivers and Bull. They occupied all of the twelfth floor, the top floor. I punched the big square button for the lift again and waited. Somewhere behind the big brushed metal doors, somewhere far below, a bell tinkled softly and I thought: At last. Here it comes.
   The lift sighed and the doors slid open silently and I started to enter. There was a tall man standing just inside of the door, to the left. I was inside before I realised it was Mr Jonathan Newby himself.
   'Well, well,' he drawled. 'We meet again . . .'

'Oh, hello,' I said. I hesitated before punching the button for the ground floor. 'I'm going down.'

'I'm coming with you,' he said. The doors slid shut. 'Only not down. Up.'

You could hardly tell the lift was moving, it was so silent and effortless. I looked at him, puzzled. 'Up? We're on the top floor already, aren't we?'

'Quite so . . . . Only there is the roof. Every house must have a roof, *n'est-ce pas*?'

The lift sighed to a halt and Mr Jonathan Newby reached for the key that he had inserted into the control board. The doors slid open.

'Please,' he said, 'after you.'

'What's this?'

'I want to have a little chat with you, Miss whatever your real name is. Snipcott's sister? I don't think so. I've just been checking with Personnel. Snipcott didn't have a sister. Now!'

Suddenly he wasn't a gentleman any longer. Which shouldn't have surprised me. That business is skin-deep oftener than not.

He caught me by the arm and, though I'm no five-stone weakling, I was no match for him physically. He pushed me into a squalid little kind of hut where the lift workings were exposed to naked view. The doors slid shut and the lift sighed away.

'Okay, what's your game? Who sent you?'

'Snipcott sent me,' I said, backing away from the big revolving wheels that carried the lift cables. 'A dead man sent me. The name's Jay Acme. Of the Acme Detective Agency.'

'You're joking.'

'Call the police. See if they laugh.'

'The police sent you?'

'I told you. Snipcott sent me.'

'You're lying. Was it those bloody City watchdogs, then?'

I shrugged. 'I see you don't want to know the truth.'

'What do you mean?'

'It was you, wasn't it, who sent Snipcott those filthy magazines . . . . You were trying to scare him. Or incriminate him. He knew too much about your crooked share deals. Isn't that what it was all about? What was the plan? Tip off the police and have him arrested? Who'd take the word of a child pervert against the wearer of the old school tie . . . ?'

A savage look transformed Newby's face for a moment. Then he smiled. 'You can't prove anything. You're full of hot air.'

I pulled out a folded brown envelope, one of the envelopes he had in his bottom drawer. 'Recognise it? It's the same cheap brand used to send the magazines to Snipcott. You've got a drawer full of them. The stuff your company uses is much better quality. That should interest the police, don't you think?'

'Anybody can buy envelopes like those. So what?'

'But not everybody can type them on your secretary's machine. You typed them yourself, didn't you, after she was gone.'

'You can't prove that.'

'Experts can. But we don't need experts,' I said. 'Just this.'

I slipped out of my handbag a spool of carbon typing ribbon.

'This is off your secretary's typewriter. The carbon's been used. Funny thing about carbon ribbons, you can read them. Did you know that? It's true. They only get used once so the used carbon ribbon can be read just like ticker tape.'

He started forward. 'Here, give me that.'

'Hold it,' I said. 'You haven't heard everything.'

'What do you mean?'

'That was a neat job on the Tube. Prodding little Mr Snipcott into oblivion with your brolly. You prodded him too hard, though. You jabbed him so hard you punctured his back. They can match the wound against your brolly. Size and shape of wound, blood type and all that. And when they do . . .'

That had floored him. I could see the way his face went pale.

'Also,' I said, 'that eyewitness remembered something. The man with the brolly was wearing one of these.'

I slid the copper rheumatism bracelet out of my pocket and held it up for him to see. His eyes closed momentarily as though in pain. 'Recognise it, Mr Newby?'

I thought for a moment he was going to faint. He didn't. He took a few deep breaths, then came at me. I was no match for him. Tai Chi classes didn't really equip you for it. I flailed at him with arms and legs but he started to overpower me.

'You're going to commit suicide,' he hissed at me through teeth clenched with exertion. 'Off the roof . . . . Balance of the mind and all that . . . .'

'You'll never get away with it,' I hissed back. I started to black out. I brought my knee up hard and he groaned. But he didn't let go of my neck.

We fell to the ground and he rolled on top of me. His hands were clasped to my throat like cords of steel.

'Oh, yes . . . ,' he murmured. 'Oh, yes . . . .'

I started to go limp. And then I heard it. The voice was pure East End. But it was the sweetest sound I'd ever heard in my life. It was coming from the lift doors, which had silently opened.

'Hey, Harry. Look at this, will you! It's a couple here. Bonking away, they are . . . .'

The two lift maintenance men had been interviewed and let go. The rest of the office had gone home. Police were busy in Mr Newby's office and Newby himself, I suppose they'd got him in a cell somewhere at the local cop shop. The Superintendent who had interviewed me at great length (with more to come) offered to have a police car drive me home. Which was gentlemanly enough. Professionals don't usually take kindly to amateurs poking their noses into serious business.

I didn't go straight home, though. I had them drop me off in Soho. San Michele was a quiet little spot and I could see why Mr Snipcott would have favoured it. I ordered *osso bucco* and a half bottle of red. When it was poured I raised the glass in a silent toast, that I thought somehow Snipcott might hear: 'To the Snipcotts! To the little people! Sometimes justice flourishes! Sometimes . . . !'

PAINT

JOAN SMITH

Joan Smith was born in London and educated at state schools and Reading University. She is a former *Sunday Times* reporter who now divides her time between journalism, broadcasting, and writing books. She is the author of two crime novels, *A Masculine Ending* and *Why Aren't They Screaming?* (Faber & Faber). She has also written a book about the British bomb tests in the 1950s, *Clouds of Deceit*. Her next book, *Misogynies*, is a series of reflections on the subject of woman-hating. She lives in north Oxfordshire.

To this day, I do my best not to think about the Stephenson job. It *should* have been a big event in my life, my working life that is, but I – well, it makes me uncomfortable just thinking about it.

I didn't dislike him at first, not at all. I was quite keen on him, in fact. It was my first big job, and I couldn't quite believe he'd taken me on, given how inexperienced I was. Looking back, it must have had something to do with what I was charging. I was so desperate to get the job that I offered him a ridiculous price – in the end, I hardly made any profit at all. I made the stupid mistake of quoting all-in terms, and then under-estimating the cost of the materials. Stippling, rag-rolling, all those decorative finishes use a lot of paint, and I had to do one room twice to get the effect I wanted. He gave me a free hand, apart from the colour schemes, and it didn't even strike me as odd that he wanted the whole place done from top to bottom. He must have realised I was pathetically grateful for the work and wouldn't ask too many questions.

Oh God, there I go again. It's not as if – well, I'll come to

111

that in a minute. First I should tell you how it came about, me doing up James Stephenson's flat. As I said, it was my first big job after I went into the decorating business, after I set myself up as a model Thatcherite enterprise, as my friend Pat rather cruelly put it. It didn't seem to me I had much choice, as I told her at the time. There was almost an element of poetic justice about it — victim of Thatcher cuts sets up small business and succeeds beyond her wildest dreams. I mean, I never thought the day would come when I'd be employing three other people. The day I collected my redundancy cheque from the council — they'd been rate-capped three years running and we in the environmental health department were just about the last to go — I was convinced I'd never earn another penny in my life. I knew the money wouldn't last long, particularly as I'd taken on a huge new mortgage just before it all happened, and I really was at my wits' end. That's why I started doing up my own flat, partly to take my mind off things, and partly because I was pretty sure I'd have to sell it and I thought a coat of paint might push up the price. I was halfway through when Pat came over. 'You ought to be doing this for a living,' she said, sounding as if she couldn't believe her eyes. 'I mean, *I* couldn't do anything as good as this. You've got a talent for it. And I bet you could make a lot of money. Look at all the skips there are round here. Houses being done up all over Islington. And they've got *money*, these people. Yuppies. They all work in the City. You'd make a bomb.'

I told her I wasn't interested in 'making a bomb'. 'Fair enough,' she said. 'But wouldn't it be nice not to have to worry about how you're going to pay the mortgage? That redundancy money won't last forever, you know.' She didn't need to tell me *that*. After she went, the idea seemed to take root in my mind. I lay in bed staring at the ceiling, arguing backwards and forwards with myself. 'It's a waste of your professional qualifications,' I pointed out sniffily, 'all those years you spent training and earning next to nothing.' On the other hand, none of my job applications to other councils in London had produced even a hint of a job. It was beginning to look like I'd have to leave London if I was going to work as an environmental health officer again, and I very much didn't want to do that. My entire social life, such as it was, was in north London

– a small area bounded by Stoke Newington in the north and the Angel in the south, in fact. 'I could give it a try,' I told myself cautiously. 'I wouldn't be committing myself to anything. If you're self-employed you can pack it in any time.' It took me ages to go to sleep and when I did I spent the night climbing ever higher ladders to paint a ceiling that seemed to be growing to the proportions of the Sistine Chapel.

I started off in a very small way, with a card in the window of two or three local newsagents. They produced a couple of small jobs, certainly nothing like enough to live on. So I got a bit bolder, and put an advert in the local paper. Nothing happened the first week. The second time it appeared, James Stephenson rang. 'I want my flat redecorated,' he said when I picked up the phone, 'and I want it done as soon as possible. How are you fixed? And what do you charge?'

'Let me just check the appointments book,' I said, thinking quickly. 'Um, let's see. This week is pretty busy, but I suppose – '

'Look, I meant what I said,' his voice cut in. 'I know what you self-employed people are like. You say Friday to get the job, and what you really mean is next Wednesday if I'm lucky. I want someone who can start this week, Thursday or Friday at the latest.'

I swallowed. 'OK. It'll mean having to put a couple of things off . . . . When can I come round to do an estimate?'

'That won't be necessary,' he said briskly. 'Just tell me what you charge. It's a largish flat, two bedrooms, living-room, kitchen and bathroom, and I want you to do the lot. And the stairs, of course.'

'Wallpaper or paint?' I asked, equally businesslike, though I could hardly believe my luck. 'I specialise in decorative paint-work, rag-rolling and that sort of thing. Is £40 a day all right?' I thought I heard him hesitate. 'That includes materials,' I added hastily.

'Done', he said. If he hadn't been at the other end of a telephone line I'd probably have kissed him.

Everything was pretty straightforward for the first two or three days. James was waiting for me at the flat when I arrived at nine-fifteen next morning; he gave me a fast tour, supplied me with a list of colours for each room, and told me to help myself to tea and coffee. The answering-machine was on, he said, so I didn't need to bother with the phone. I was grateful for that, as it turned out that it rang a lot. I did wonder why all these people weren't ringing him at work, but I'll come to that later. He was just as I'd pictured him from his voice on the phone – late twenties, posh background, job in the City (something to do with commodities, he told me, but I didn't really take it in). I tuned his wildly expensive stereo system to Radio Four and set to work.

He seemed to leave the house pretty early in the mornings – I didn't see him again until I arrived at the flat on Monday, when we collided at the front door. 'Must dash,' he said, flashing me a brief smile and rushing past to the white Porsche parked two or three doors up the street. I hauled tins of paint upstairs to the flat – it was a maisonette on the top two floors of a three-storey Victorian house – and let myself in. I hadn't been there long when someone rapped at the front door. Resting my brush across the top of a tin of paint I went to open it, wondering how whoever it was had got past the main door of the house on the ground floor.

'Judy? Oh.' The woman standing outside looked terribly disappointed. 'Sorry, I thought Judy was back . . . .'

'I'm just the decorator,' I said apologetically. 'I'm afraid I don't know any Judy. Have you got the right flat?'

'*Of course* I've got the right flat!' the woman said indignantly. 'I live downstairs. I think I've been here long enough to know who my neighbours are! D'you mean Judy hasn't come back?' By now her attitude was positively belligerent.

'I'm sorry,' I apologised again, 'I don't know who this Judy is. I've been coming here since last Tuesday and there's only ever been me here. Apart from Mr Stephenson, that is. And I've only seen him once. He's out at work all day.'

'Yes, I know that,' she said irritably. She was tall and fair, with short hair and a single ear-ring dangling from one ear; the sort of person that I might have taken to in other circumstances, but not if she persisted in being as unfriendly as this. 'What's all this about decorating the flat?' she demanded suddenly. 'It's the first I've heard of it.'

I might have said that there didn't seem to be any reason

why James Stephenson should consult his neighbours before doing something to his own flat, but I didn't. I'm glad I held back, with hindsight. She was in exactly the same position as I was about to be – except that she knew Judy and I didn't.

'Look,' she said again. 'I didn't mean to sound rude. It's just that Judy, she's James's wife, went off suddenly a couple of weeks ago and I haven't seen or heard of her since. Surely he's mentioned her?'

'No,' I said, shaking my head. 'To be honest, I thought he lived here on his own.'

'You mean her things – her things are gone?' The woman's eyes were fixed on me, as though I'd said something highly significant.

'Well I . . . I haven't been looking, if you see what I mean. I had no idea she was supposed to be here, so I didn't really take in – '

'Let's have a look upstairs,' she said, moving forwards as if to push me out of the way.

Feeling extremely awkward, I barred her way. 'Wait a minute, I don't think – I mean, I have to think about Mr Stephenson . . .'

'And what about Judy? What about her?'

'Maybe she – maybe she went on holiday?'

'That's what he said. She was fed up with her job and decided to take a holiday.'

'Well then – '

'But she wasn't fed up with her job. She loved it. It was him she was fed up with, him and his – '

'I'm sorry,' I said, feeling tremendously uncomfortable, 'but I don't think I should be talking to you like this. Mr Stephenson is my employer.'

She looked at me for a second, then stepped back. 'I see – more than your job's worth,' she said sarcastically, turning to go downstairs. 'Thanks *very* much.' A moment later I heard a door slam.

It wouldn't be true to say that I was unaffected by this conversation, but I did do my best to put it out of my mind. James Stephenson had so far been a model employer, even offering me quite a large amount of cash in advance, and it seemed perfectly plausible that his wife had gone off on one of those cheap holidays you can get at 48 hours' notice. Perhaps that was why he wanted the flat done quickly – to surprise her when she got back. I just hoped that, if this was what had happened, she'd like the way I was doing it. It did seem funny, though, that when I next happened to look in the main bedroom, the one with James Stephenson's pyjamas lying untidily on the bed, there was no sign of a woman's bits and pieces anywhere in the room – no make-up, no half-empty bottles of perfume, none of the jewellery and stuff I tend to leave lying around at home. I wondered if they'd had a row and she'd left him; men can be funny about things like that. When Pat walked out on her boyfriend before last, the dim blonde one, he didn't tell anyone she'd gone for months. She only found out when someone rang up to say she was sorry Pat hadn't been able to come to dinner with Jerry, six weeks after they'd split up. I did have a peek in the wardrobe, and I couldn't see any women's clothes, which sort of supported my idea that she'd gone for good. I don't know why, but I didn't mention any of this to the fair girl from downstairs when I met her in the hall next morning. Actually, she was quite rude to me. 'Any sign of Judy?' she inquired abruptly. 'Or is it a state secret?' I shook my head and maintained a dignified silence.

Later that week – the Thursday, I suppose it was – I wished I'd been more forthcoming. I arrived at the flat slightly late, and the phone was ringing. It stopped as I walked through the door, and I assumed the machine had answered it. When it rang an hour or so later, it went on and on and I suddenly realised James had forgotten to set the machine. I flung down my brush, rushed into the main bedroom to answer it, and tried to read the number upside down. '609-er . . . .' I got out, when a voice cut in.

'Mrs Stephenson? At *last*. I've been trying to get you for days. How are you? Your husband – '

'No,' I interrupted, 'I'm not her. She's not here, I mean. I'm just the decorator.'

'The decorator?' The voice had become frosty. 'Oh, I see. I don't suppose you can help me then. I'm calling from Thigh High in Upper Street, we were just wondering when Mrs Stephenson was going to be back at work. *If* she is coming back to work. Her husband told us she'd gone off on holiday for a week, but it's nearly three now and she still hasn't shown up. The shop's very busy, I can't really hold the job open for her much longer.'

'I'm sorry,' I said weakly, 'all I can do is take a message.'

'Hmmph,' the voice responded. 'I've been leaving them on that damned machine for days. If you could ask Mr Stephenson . . .'

'I hardly ever see him,' I told her firmly, 'but I'll leave a note.' I was quite anxious to get her off the phone, not liking the sound of all this. I wanted time to think, and I couldn't do it with that bossy voice bending my ear.

I wondered about going downstairs to talk to the fair woman, but I still felt very torn. People do go off without warning, and the little I'd seen of James Stephenson was enough to show me he was the repressed public-school type who probably wouldn't be up to coping with his wife walking out on him. Perhaps he was ignoring the whole thing in the hope that she'd come back. Men do that. I prowled around the flat a bit, feeling as guilty as hell, and it was while I was poking about in the small bedroom that I found the suitcase. It was under the bed, in a place where I had no business to be looking, and I felt pretty bad about opening it up. I did though, and found it contained a jumble of women's things – a jewellery box with some nice pieces in it, nothing wildly expensive but stuff that looked like it came from somewhere posh off Bond Street, Butler & Wilson maybe. There was nothing really startling, no passport or driving licence or anything like that, but there was a building society book with several hundred pounds in it. It seemed odd that she'd go off without that, unless she had loads of money in her current account as well. Which was possible, given James Stephenson's obvious affluence, the Porsche and stereo and so on. So I wasn't any further on, really. It did seem odd that this was the only evidence that she'd ever been in the flat, but then again she might have cleared out in a hurry and overlooked these bits and pieces. The only other thing of interest was a wedding picture in a silver frame, James Stephenson and a woman in a posh white dress smiling cheerfully into the camera. I don't know anything about wedding dresses, so I had no idea whether it was fashionable or not, or how recently it had been taken.

So I carried on with the job, moving into the bathroom which was the room I'd left till last. I was going to start with the ceiling, but the whole room was a bit scruffy and I thought I'd give it a clean first. Not part of my job, I know, but it hardly seems worth going to a lot of trouble with paint when the bath needs a good clean and there are those horrible drip marks on the loo. Anyway I was used to it by now; the whole flat needed a damn good clean and I'd been more or less doing each room as I went along. So I got a bowl of soapy water and a cloth and started with the loo, and it was then I noticed the marks. Well, they weren't so much marks as a kind of deposit. Oh dear, I'm not explaining this very well. I wasn't actually washing the floor, it was surprisingly clean already, but I was on my hands and knees and I happened to look down. The floor was tiled, you see, with those rather horrible plasticky things that used to be fashionable before people got into cork. And this stuff, this deposit, was in the cracks between the tiles. Sort of rust-coloured, it was, as if something had been spilt in front of the loo and along the side of the bath. I scraped my fingernail along one of the cracks and this sort of reddish gunge came up – paint, I told myself, it was obviously paint. But who uses red paint in a bathroom? I mean someone might, but not in this bathroom. It hadn't been painted for years, and the colour scheme I was about to cover up was a rather dirty shade of green. I really did panic for a moment, picturing all sorts of dark deeds, not to mention James deciding to have the flat decorated in a desperate attempt to wipe out the memory of what he'd done, and then I decided my imagination was running away with me. The stuff on the floor didn't have to be – well, human in origin, and even if it was, there might still be a simple explanation. There was a small wash-stand in the corner with a lot of shaving stuff on it, including a nasty-looking razor, and on the morning I started at the flat I'd half noticed that James seemed to have several messy cuts on his face. The simplest thing was to hang around till he came home that evening on the pretext of passing on the message from the shop. It was the perfect excuse, and he could hardly avoid answering if I raised the subject of his wife directly. On the other hand, if he had – no, I told myself firmly, there really was no evidence at all that Judy Stephenson had done anything but walk out on her husband and he was too ashamed to admit it.

When it got to half-past six and there was still no sign of James I began to get worried. I couldn't hang about the place all evening. At seven I was just putting my stuff in a neat pile when I heard his key in the door. 'Hello,' I called brightly. 'I'm just leaving.' I came out of the bathroom and down the stairs, slinging my bag over my shoulder. 'I'd got to a tricky bit and I was quite keen to finish,' I lied, nervous shivers running down my spine. Now that James was standing in front of me, looking slightly put out, my plan didn't seem so brilliant. I moved past him to the door, pulled it open, then paused stagily just inside the flat. 'Oh, by the way. You, er, forgot to put the answering-machine on. I think I've got it working for you. But there was one message, before the machine was on, I mean. A woman from a shop in Upper Street . . . she was ringing about your wife. About her job. She wanted to know when she was coming back. They're very busy, apparently, and she can't hold it open forever. She said she'd been trying to get hold of you to ask when .. to ask whether . . . ' His silence was making me gabble. 'Oh, and the woman downstairs, I don't know her name, she was asking about her as well.'

James was frowning. 'Blast, I assumed Judy would get in . . . oh well, I'll deal with it. Thanks very much,' he said shortly, waiting for me to go.

'Don't mention it,' I said stupidly, smiling and nodding like an idiot. What had he meant to say? That he had expected his wife to do her own dirty work? He certainly didn't seem nervous or afraid, just put out, as if the subject was one he didn't want to deal with. 'I'll be off then.' I started down the stairs, and was halted halfway by his voice, stern and cold.

'By the way, Verity – how much longer do you need? Any chance of having it done by tomorrow?'

I was taken aback. 'Well, I *had* thought – I was planning to get it all done by Monday. If that's all right with you.'

'But there's only the bathroom left, surely? If you made an early start you could have it finished by tomorrow evening? It's the smell, you see, I don't like the smell of paint.'

'Well, I suppose . . . all right.' I was feeling put out now, grumpy at the thought of losing an extra day's pay.

'If it's the money that's bothering you, don't worry. Charge me for Monday as well. In fact, you'd better bring your bill with you when you come tomorrow. Leave it on the kitchen table and I'll put a cheque in the post. Bye.'

He closed the door, and that was the last time I saw James Stephenson. Even though I turned up early next morning, around half past eight, he had already gone. A plate covered in toast crumbs and a half-full cup of coffee on the kitchen table were the only signs that he'd been there until very recently. That, and four birthday cards standing in a row next to the plate as though they'd just arrived. I have to admit curiosity got the better of me, and I looked at them one by one, trying not to disturb their position on the table. There was one with a racing car on the front – 'Much love from Mum and Dad'; two with pictures of flowers, from 'Robin' and 'Susie and Dick' respectively; and there was a photo of a cat curled up on the keyboard of a piano which had been signed with a flourish – 'A big hug from Judy'.

I was so relieved I had to sit down. You've been a proper Charlie, I told myself – just think what would have happened if you'd gone rushing downstairs with your wild theories. Or, even worse, to the police. 'A big hug from Judy.' Whatever their problem had been, it looked as if James and Judy were well on the way to sorting it out. I plonked my bill on the table, breathed a huge sigh of relief at the thought of my narrow escape, and went to work with a vengeance. The bathroom was all done by just after four – brilliant, the best room in the house. I really put my heart and soul into it. I felt it was the least I could do.

I didn't give James or Judy Stephenson another thought for ages, not once the cheque had cleared. But some time later, three or four months after I'd finished the flat, I happened to drive down their road. I noticed a furniture van parked halfway down, and when I got nearer I saw two men in overalls carrying a sofa I recognised out of the front door. They were followed by a man with a tea-chest, and a woman with short black hair who seemed to be directing operations. It was a warm day and I had the window down; I saw the woman turn and go back into the house, and I distinctly heard one of the men call her name: 'Mrs Stephenson'. I was so astonished I nearly crashed the car. I was past them by this time, so I pulled up and waited for her to come out of the house. I saw her clearly in my rear-view mirror before I drove on; tall and dark, nothing like the petite, brown-haired woman in the wedding photograph. And then I thought of the way he'd hurried me out of the flat as soon as I mentioned his wife, and the birthday cards standing on the table where I'd be bound to see them, and I remembered that there weren't any envelopes lying nearby where you'd expect them to be. And I thought, God knows when his birthday really was. But you can see why, ever since, I've tried never to think about the Stephenson job.

AN ACCIDENT IN NEPAL

CHRIS WATT

Chris Watt was born and educated in Edinburgh, but has lived and worked in both England and Wales, latterly as a civil servant. She is at present living with her husband and two daughters overlooking the banks of the silvery Tay. She loathes having her photograph taken.

The Himalayan night is a thick blackness hiding my hand held in front of my face, pressing solidly against my open, unseeing eyes. Above the steady rhythm of Richard's breathing, I can hear the wind sighing along the ridge. Only a thin layer of canvas between me and the vast mountains watching outside. I fight sleep, parading against the darkness the occupants of the other tents in the circle. Tony and Marge Van Buren, the Leclercs, Adrian Trent. And Richard and me. Have I caught a glimpse of the truth, or is this a child's fantasy, a sombre fairy tale woven out of my own sickness of heart? Was the girl murdered, was it one of us? I visualise Marge Van Buren lying awake too, turning that little silver packet between her fingers. I am sure of nothing, sure of no one. In the whirl of thought, not even of Richard – that is the final dread; that I cannot even put my husband above suspicion. And then, sometime in the black hours, I remember – Richard and Tony Van Buren left together, early in the morning. They alibi each other. An end to this arguing and counter-arguing. There was no murder, my mind deceives me. Finally, sleep.

Mrs Van Buren and I were thrown together from the first morning, because we walked at the same pace. Richard and Tony Van Buren went striding on, but she was happy to stay with me till I finished drawing. A wonderful Nepali house, with elaborate, almost medieval, carving on the shutters had caught my eye, just on the outskirts of Pokhara itself. When I looked up and found we were alone, she caught my frown.

'Never take them too seriously, Jan honey, they're only men – you don't mind if I call you Jan, do you? You just call me Marge – You gotta allow for their handicaps, sweetheart. Given their hormones we'd be bustin' a gut trying to keep up with the Gurkhas too.' I laughed, it seemed for the first time in weeks, and took more careful stock of her. Above those riveting black and white checked trousers she was a trim woman, middle-aged in that well-preserved American way, teeth her own, hair a perfect gold. And under all that, a glint that defied the word matronly.

For most of that morning the French couple, the Leclercs, kept up more or less the same speed as us, but seemed to make a point of avoiding intimacy, quickening their pace as we neared them. After the second time that happened, Mrs Van Buren (I couldn't easily think of her as Marge) said, 'Funny bunch, the French.' It's easy when you're travelling in Asia, meeting perhaps only one or two people of other nationalities, to slip into these blanket generalisations. 'Is her name Francine, or what? How come he keeps calling her Chantal?' How come indeed. For ever after, my image of the entire French nation has been coloured by the Leclercs – ambiguous, unconvincing, Chantal/Francine in her pre-Raphaelite draperies.

Adrian, the other Englishman, we passed and repassed all day. He would lope past us, somehow managing to seem preoccupied and ingratiating at one and the same time, only to be overtaken again crawling among the scrubby bushes as some specimen caught his eye. 'Of course, you English are the great gardeners of the world,' said Mrs Van Buren. I hoped her image of 'the English' wouldn't contain too much of Adrian Trent.

For most of the day our route wound up the river valley, bare stony shoulders rising on either side. A desolate landscape, little tiered layers of green chipped out of it around clusters of houses here and there. Bare brown children accosted us as we passed, familiar with the ways and possible generosity of tourists. Then in the afternoon the track swung across a rickety wooden suspension bridge and rose sharply up the hill opposite.

'Oh my God, do we go up there?' Mrs Van Buren craned back to follow the loops of the path, so steep in places that steps had been cut, winding in and out of stands of bamboo and rhododendron trees. 'Time to break out the candy. What we need is blood sugar.' She produced from her shoulder bag a purple and white bar at once familiar and unfamiliar.

'"Manufactured by Cadbury India Limited."' Reading that aloud I was swamped by a wave of homesickness.

'You been out of England long, honey?'

'Too long I sometimes think – three months.'

'I guess it depends what you leave behind. Myself, I don't miss any of it. Small-town America, Jan, that's what Tony and me got out of – the bitching, the finger-pointing. Someone whispers behind your back, you've had it. Trial by gossip.' I was surprised out of my own self-pity by the hardness of her tone and face. What on earth could small-town America have judged this nice woman guilty of? There was an awkward little silence, until a mule train clopped down the steps and past us onto the bridge.

'Namas-te,' roared the drivers, friendly and good-natured.

'Namas-te,' we bowed back, remembering our manners, then I grabbed for my sketch pad.

'I just love those plumes and mirrors they put on the little mules for head-dresses, don't you Jan? You think Nato knows you can ward off the evil eye with some feathers and painted glass?' I laughed again. The bad memory, whatever it was, was gone. 'C'mon honey, let's finish this candy. We can always get our asses lifted later.'

Running footsteps sounded above us, and Ang Dawa came leaping into view, two steps at a time. 'Ah, ladies, my ladies. You are tired? Not far now. The tents will be just up here.' He waved loosely at a point perhaps 2,000 feet above. 'I carry you, yes?'

'You carry me, no.' Mrs Van Buren rapped his knuckles. 'Keep your mitts to yourself. We're doin' just fine.' He grinned. This was his kind of woman.

What did he make of us all, I wondered, plodding up those thigh-aching steps, my eyes on the bouncing soles of his boots.

Presumably for a Sherpa versed in the eccentricities of tourists, we all fell into recognisable types. Competitive, like Richard and Tony Van Buren, woolly like the Leclercs, wet like Adrian, tough but warm like Mrs Van Buren. Homesick, like me. Just a tail-end of the season, fag-end of a trekking party, bound for the eternal flames of Muktinath. No doubt he'd seen it all before.

A corner revealed yet another bank of steps, and halfway up a slight figure sitting against one of the big conical Nepali baskets. It was one of our girl porters, nursing her foot in her hands. I had noticed her in the morning at Pokhara, because to Western eyes she was so pretty – Nepalis have these wonderful facial bones. Ang Dawa ahead of us burst into quick furious Nepali. The girl lowered her eyes and said nothing.

'What's up?' Mrs Van Buren sat on the step beside me. 'Boy, am I glad to sit down.'

'Is nothing. No problem.' Another barrage of Nepali. I knelt on the step below and moved her hands aside.

'Shit!' Mrs Van Buren went white on the intake of breath. Across the fleshy pad of the heel a long gash seeped dark blood. 'I've got some Bandaid, honey. Can you do something with it? I'm no good at this.'

'It really needs stitches. But I could fasten the plaster across it to hold the edges of the skin together.' I took the wad of tissues Mrs Van Buren supplied. They were startlingly pastel against the thickened brown skin of the girl's foot. 'But how can we keep it clean when she's not wearing shoes?'

'Hold it, hold it.' From the magic shoulder bag she produced a pair of bright pink, polka-dotted canvas shoes. 'You can have these, sweetheart. I only brought them in case my boots hurt, and they've been OK.'

'For me?' The dark eyes devoured the shoes.

'Sure. But they might be kinda big. Watch you don't fall.'

'Nepalis not fall.' When she stood up, glowing with pleasure, she seemed barely more than a pretty child, her body slight under her dusty cotton jacket and long skirt. The bright plimsolls were incongruous below. She bowed in thanks over folded hands, then backed into the shoulder straps of her basket, adjusted her headband and scampered ahead up the steps with a bright sideways glance at Ang Dawa's impatience. She appeared to have no trace of a limp.

Ang Dawa gave a little appreciative jerk of head and eyebrows. 'You nurse?'

'No, no.' But as I fell into step with Mrs Van Buren behind him, I felt how pleasant it was to be good at something for a change. If I had guessed the heartache to be caused by my status as medical officer, I should have been less pleased with myself.

That first night the tents were pitched just below a village, in a stubble field perched between the path and a steep drop down to the river. As we two trudged over the last rise, the others were just sitting down at the trestle tables. Behind and above spread our first clear view of the Himalayas. Those tantalising white glimpses we had had from Pokhara were now fleshed out, become huge icy bulwarks floating in mists. To me they were inimical, awesome. To set foot on such perfection would be upstart irreverence.

'I hope you're not going to lag behind all the way to Muktinath,' Richard greeted me. I noticed his nose was beginning to peel.

'Hey, Richie, be nice to her. Remember this is the gentler sex.' With an arm round Marge's shoulders, Tony Van Buren showed his white even teeth at me. At that moment he became the focus of everything I was feeling, about the mountains, about Richard, about Nepali girls carrying upwards of forty pounds, about being a parasite tourist. I have seldom disliked anyone more.

As I ate, Richard spread his map on the table beside me. 'Tony and I are leaving early tomorrow, before breakfast. We can set our own pace for Gorepani, there's a point above there where you can get the first clear view of Annapurna. Tony reckons we can knock an hour at least off the time the guide-book gives.'

'Goodness.' I said it without expression.

'What's the matter with you?'

'Do you like Tony Van Buren?'

'He used to be a first-class athlete, you know. Just missed the '72 Olympics.' He lowered his voice. 'I don't know how he can stand that awful woman.'

I looked up the table. Tony was between his wife and the French girl. Marge's face was animated; every so often she

126

touched him, as if she couldn't help herself. A hand on his, her cheek brushed against his shoulder. Seeing them together like that I realised for the first time there must be several years' difference in their ages.

Suddenly the French girl pushed away her plate, stood up and said something emphatic to Tony. Then she swung away from the table. 'Chan ... Francine!' As she didn't turn, her husband too pushed back his chair and followed her. Tony Van Buren caught my eye and mimed innocent incomprehension. I looked away.

'Too much hashish is my bet,' opined Mrs Van Buren later in the women's wash tent. I mumbled something non-committal. 'Weird people altogether, those two. Hell, I'm no prude but you don't have to go flashing pubic hair when there's *cubicles*.' From behind her own hessian curtain came the hiss of an aerosol and waves of expensive perfume. 'I looked for our little Nepali after supper, honey, but Ang Dawa says the porters went to eat in the village.'

In our tent Richard was stowing a packet of bread and boiled eggs in his haversack. He opened his guide-book. 'We drop right down to below 4,000 feet straight away tomorrow, then climb more or less all day from there.' I turned my face into my pillow and thought about how even the toughest, smartest women, like Mrs Van Buren, can be crippled by emotions. Then I remembered her philosophy. 'You gotta allow for their handicaps.' I fell asleep smiling.

In the morning the mountains were paling from scarlet as I left the tent, and I joined the Leclercs at the edge of the field. Chantal/Francine was still in a transparent nightdress and barefoot.

'Magnifique, non?'

I nodded. 'The very roof of the world.'

'Can you guys turn to me a little? You're just neat for the foreground interest.' Marge Van Buren crouched to one side of us, wielding her camera.

'Non!' said Chantal, 'Non, non, non! Paul, viens-toi!' And crab-like, faces turned from the camera, they edged away across the field.

Mrs Van Buren straightened up, dumbfounded. 'Is it me or

them, honey? Do you reckon they can have altitude sickness? I thought he was called Jean?'

Ang Dawa rounded us up. 'Breakfast time. Tsampa and toast. You like tsampa? Kind of porridge.'

'Today I like everything Ang Dawa.' I sniffed deeply. 'Just looking at the mountains makes me ravenous. Do you know what time the wunderkinds left, Marge?'

'No, honey, it was before I opened an eye.'

The tents were struck before we finished eating, and the first porters started off up the track. 'No dreaming,' chivvied Ang Dawa, 'Long walk today.'

But as we gathered our bags and prepared to leave the emptying field, a hubbub arose among the remaining porters. Two baskets lay propped against each other, unclaimed. Ang Dawa looked thunderous. Then a shout from the edge of the stubble field made us turn. A porter stood on the far side, where the Leclercs and I had been earlier, pointing urgently down towards the river. Something below had caught his eye.

'What's wrong, Ang Dawa?'

'An accident, only an accident. Please,' he ushered the rest of the group towards the track with his hands, 'Continue. I deal. Mrs Jan, Mrs Marge, you come please?' Our prowess in first aid was remembered.

The slope down to the river was steep and wooded, the path overgrown. We followed Ang Dawa and the porter, stumbling from foothold to foothold, clutching at branches, bamboo spiking our legs. And all the way I worried at my inadequate skills for dealing with a serious accident.

I need not have worried. She was already quite dead. Her body lay face down in the gentle shallows at the river's edge, as if resting on the sandy gravel. The current that roared by tugged playfully at the cotton of her skirt. Our little Nepali girl was no longer pretty. Unasked, my mind offered a picture of her body being smashed from rock to rock. Her face was dreadfully disfigured, all her neck and shoulders bruised, and her hands . . . It is not something I wish to remember, even now. Only the pink shoes identified her beyond doubt.

They lifted her body onto a kind of litter they made from branches, and covered her with a jacket. But those sad, bright shoes stuck stiffly out from one side. Mrs Van Buren and I were together behind them as they left the river bank, a silent, shocked procession. Just at the first trees I saw her bend and pick something from between two rocks. It was a little silver sachet of salt, the kind supplied by air-lines with in-flight meals. I had some myself in my bag. It is the kind of thing that can be useful on a trek.

Once back in the empty stubble field, Ang Dawa sent us on to catch up with the others, and take his instructions about the next camp. Then he and the porter set off back down the steps, the stretcher bumping awkwardly behind, and the pink shoes . . . . But that is enough.

Almost an hour passed before either of us spoke. At last we stopped to fill our water bottles at a little stream piped under the track, and as I bent to the water the sound of it gurgling downhill brought that image back again. I put a hand over my eyes. 'I just can't stop seeing her. She was so . . . so . . .' Marge supplied a bundle of tissues again, and put an arm around my shoulders.

'We should talk about it, sweetheart.'

'She was so alive.' I blew my nose but the tears continued uninterrupted. Marge's cheeks were wet too. 'One day so pretty and bright. Those shoes, she was so pleased with them. And her poor legs were so stiff . . .' Marge put both arms around me and we just stood, close together. How comforting it can be to have another human being so close; alive and holding you. In a little while we washed our faces in the stream and walked on. I didn't say anything about the little packet of salt. It was something I would think about later.

We camped that night near a village called Hille, a sober evening, the altitude making it cold and even Tony and Richard's enthusiasm for record-breaking dimmed by the events of the day. Ang Dawa arrived as light was fading, grim and disinclined to chat. No one had much appetite for the evening meal.

'But what actually happened, Ang Dawa? How did she die?' Adrian asked it finally, self-importantly, aware of the Leclercs hanging behind him, and of the rest of us listening for the answer too.

'An accident, is all. Washing in morning, maybe dizzy, maybe slip. Who knows?' Then he scowled and took the offensive. 'You not dig plants today, I hope?' Adrian blushed and retreated. To the Leclercs Ang Dawa said, 'Something wrong? You got problem?' Whatever irony they detected in that, it had the effect of silencing them too.

We all retired to our own tents early that night. And as the lights were dimmed and the subdued murmurs faded, I lay unsleeping, playing patience in my head with a pack of marked cards. The bruises on her throat. The sachet of salt. No more. In the dark small hours, no less. I remember the relief when I realised that Tony and Richard, thanks to their early start, provided each other with alibis. And the guilt that followed.

The next morning came through cloud, cold and dispirited, everyone seemed pale and withdrawn. When we set out the groupings had changed, in that the Van Burens walked together, Richard stayed with me, and some sort of alliance seemed to have formed between Adrian and the Leclercs. That day after an initial steep climb, the track led us down again through thin woods, ablaze now and then with bright blossoms of rhododendron. Across the valley hung walls of white.

'I don't know why you don't draw something like that,' said Richard once, pointing to a glow of red flowers against distant snows, 'instead of all these grubby children.'

'I can't do landscapes. I like things that live and breathe best.' As I said it, I remembered the dead Nepali girl, and the terrible waste of it.

'Look, forget it, Jan.' Richard was definite. 'It has nothing to do with us. Remember this is our trip of a lifetime. Don't spoil it by getting worked up about how the other half lives, or dies.'

Not long after midday we stopped by a stream to eat lunch and for Richard to bathe his feet. The route march with Tony the day before had left him with blisters.

'Hey, that looks a great idea.' The Van Burens were walking hand in hand, but now Marge too was limping. 'I swear I have a boulder the size of Annapurna itself in my boot, but I cannot find it.' But when she took off her boot and sock, the weave of the yarn was printed in the weeping surface of a burst blister.

'Oh, heavens, that must be sore. Let me put a plaster on it for you.'

'I'll bathe it first, honey. Oh-h-h! That is just wonderful. I guess my boots aren't as good a fit as I thought at first.'

'Well, if you hadn't given away those God-awful sneakers, you could've put them on.' Tony stood above us, hands on slim hips.

I looked up as Marge flinched and saw her pale. 'I'm sorry, am I being too rough?'

'I'm OK, honey, carry on.'

After that we four walked together on to the next campsite.

'Tomorrow is easy day,' promised Ang Dawa when we got there. 'Only one "kos" to Tatopani, we spend morning here. And tomorrow in evening – hot baths!' There were general sighs of longing and anticipation – none I think more heartfelt than mine. My last bath had been a month ago, a lukewarm affair in a tin-lined bath in Sri Lanka. Showers are all very well, but not the same.

'You're not kidding about these hot springs at Tatopani, Ang Dawa?'

He looked pained. 'No, no. Is truth. Tatopani means "hot water". Two springs, you will see. Tourists like very much.'

In the morning the atmosphere of the group had relaxed again. So much lower, the air was warmer and softer, the horror of the girl's death was receding. My suspicions, like the cold of Hille, seemed a long way behind. After breakfast the Leclercs retreated to their tent, and when presently there issued the now familiar sweet smell, Ang Dawa made a wry comment in his idiosyncratic English that set the rest of us laughing, drawn together by the French couple's oddness. Adrian crawled happily into the undergrowth around the tents. I sketched most of the morning. I have a rather sarcastic impression of Richard gingerly pulling a sock on his blistered foot. Then there is a drawing of three porters squatting by the fire, smoking those poisonous little brown 'bidis'. Tony Van Buren lolls behind them, wrinkling his perfect nose at the smoke – Tony didn't approve of smoking, not good for the body beautiful. And the best sketch I did, perhaps have ever done, is of Marge and Ang Dawa together, unaware of me, deep in conversation. Both strong faces, and yet so different. East meeting West.

Lunch was a leisurely affair, and with the eternal 'chai' afterwards came a treat, little nutty cakes soaked in syrup that Ang Dawa had procured from a village.

'A million calories in every bite, honey,' said Marge, 'Here, Tony, you have mine too. I got the one with the pistachio or whatever on top. I ain't so nutty I'm going to eat it,' she patted her flat stomach, 'I'm not going to rub out the effects of three days' walking.'

The porters set off for Tatopani while we drank our tea and a festive atmosphere infected the group, as if we were mere picnickers on a summer jaunt. Even the Leclercs sat in the circle as we teased Ang Dawa. 'How far to Tatopani, Ang Dawa? One "kos"? But one of your "koses" is worth six of mine.'

He laid a hand on his heart. 'Only stroll, Mrs Jan, I promise. After bridge, is nothing.'

'The bridge?'

'Not very good bridge. Landslide take good bridge away. But – take care – is nothing.'

As with all of Ang Dawa's descriptions, this proved to be less than full. When we came to the edge of the gorge, and looked down, there were gasps and mutters from all of us. The 'bridge' consisted of thin branches lashed to two ropes slung across the chasm. Even to a casual glance the ropes were old and frayed. Another rope, suspended at waist height, provided the only handrail.

'Is not difficult, hold this,' Ang Dawa demonstrated. 'And look up, up, never down. I show.' He stepped on and the bridge undulated under his weight. He walked to the middle and then, forty feet above the rushing water below, calmly bent and seemed to retie a bootlace. Next to me Francine gasped, and I felt my own stomach heave. Then from the other side, holding the handrail steady, Ang Dawa called, 'See? No problem. First one – Mr Tony, you show.'

'Sure. Should I do it on my head, or just with one hand tied behind my back?' As he laughed, I remember thinking what a pain the man is. Then suddenly I saw the scene as if from a long way off, like a set piece of theatre viewed from a seat in the gods. Ang Dawa waiting at one end of the frail link, Marge at the other, the little group of tourists clustered around her like a Greek chorus. And in the middle, the fading golden boy. Part of the way across he stopped in imitation of Ang Dawa's effect, and bounced experimentally. The whole length of the bridge rippled in sequence. 'Yahoo!' he called, 'This is really something!'

'Go on, honey,' said Marge softly. Tony pranced forward, hardly using the handrail, sure of foot and perfectly balanced. And then – who could say what happened? Over-confidence? Dizziness? A stumble on an uneven branch? He clutched towards the handrail, but it was, somehow, out of reach, his balance was lost. Between one breath and the next, with no sound at all, Tony Van Buren plunged down into the jumble of rocks and white water so many feet below. Francine screamed and covered her eyes. Adrian said, 'My God!' And I . . . God help me, I was printing the scene on my mind, so that later I could draw it.

The French couple were undecided about whether to go back with us or not, but in the end only Mrs Van Buren and I, with two porters, turned back from Tatopani. Richard took my decision with equanimity. 'I'll see you in Pokhara then, Jan. In not much more than a week. I'll probably go ahead on my own and make better time. Then we'll be off to Kashmir.'

'No,' I said, 'I'm flying home.' His resistance was no more than token.

Along the trek back to Pokhara, we spoke little, Mrs Van Buren and I, and until the final day didn't mention Tony at all. We stopped on the edge of the last foothill above Pokhara, the town with its lake lay smudged in the haze below. Out of nothing she said, 'Something about these mountains.' I looked over. A trim, middle-aged woman in black and white trousers. A lot of living in her face. She was looking back towards the huge shapes now only suggested under the clouds. 'You see the bare bones, the certainties.'

'Yes, things become clear.' I flicked away an ant and sat down on a rock. A breath. 'The hashish in the cake – did you get it from the French couple?' She didn't look surprised.

'No, honey. Ang Dawa got it for me. From someone in a village.'

'And the bridge?'

'I don't know exactly. Something cut, or he loosened something. Loosened I guess, since we all crossed afterwards. I didn't ask.'

'You were certain?'

She turned away for a moment, and then sat down beside me. 'I was – am – sure.' She held out her hand and looked at the rings on her fingers. 'There was a girl before. Back home. She was beaten badly, but she survived. I believed him that time. She didn't ever testify, you see. Her parents took her to Europe.' In the silence I watched the ant crawl back up the rock.

'But that's only . . .'

'Yeah, I know. And at first I thought, but he was off at dawn with your Richard, and Ang Dawa said she had slipped in the morning.' She sighed. 'But then I remembered the shoes,' her voice almost failed. 'How the shoes stuck out from under the cover. Rigor had set in. She was killed the evening before. Somehow they didn't miss her.'

'But that still only means he *could* have done it. So could any one of us. The Leclercs – look at them . . .' She waved me down.

'You've been too long out of Europe. Though it took me a while too. Francine Leclerc is Chantal Dubois.' It still took seconds before I recognised the name.

'Then Jean is Paul Duval? Her mother's . . .?'

'Right. And one thing I do know is no one escaping from that kind of notoriety goes looking for more trouble.'

'Adrian Trent, then.' She didn't even both to answer that. 'Don't you need something more before you turn judge, jury and executioner?'

Her mouth twisted. 'The shoes, Jan. I didn't tell him about the shoes. He knew I had given them away because he saw her wearing them. When he killed her.'

I left Mrs Van Buren in Katmandu. It seemed the paperwork for the embassy would keep her there another few days. I had made my statement. My statement about the accident. There was nothing to keep me in Nepal. At the end of the week I flew home to England. One image haunted me all the way, haunts me even now, though less often as time goes on. A narrow bridge set high above a rocky river bed. A Sherpa, stocky and unsmiling at one end, Marge Van Buren at the other. And the golden boy, clowning to his death, between them.

I never saw any of them again, except once, in Birmingham's New Street station, I caught a glimpse of Richard. The young woman with him was his second wife, I think. He was, after all, the marrying kind.

SELECTED TITLES

LONDON PARTICULAR
by Christianna Brand

A car crawls through fog-bound London. Its
passengers, a middle-aged doctor, and his anxious
female friend, are responding to a call from a dying
man. But this man is not dying from any sort of
illness, it seems more like murder!

Christianna Brand, author of *Green for Danger*, has
produced another brilliant atmospheric tale set in a
smog-bound London.

Pandora Women Crime Writers Classic Crime
LC8 254pp
Paperback 0–86358–273–7

AMATEUR CITY
by Katherine V. Forrest

A modern whodunnit, in the best traditions of the
genre.
'"Please look at me Miss O'Neil." Kate Delafield sat
with arms crossed, elbows resting on the table. Her
light blue eyes were not cold, they were not hostile,
but they bored into Ellen's as if she were seeing all
the way to the back of her head. "There was a reason
why a murderer got across that hallway to safety, why
you never saw who it was."'
Kate Delafield, tough leader of the homicide
investigation team, soon discovers strong motives for
the killing of Fergus Parker in an office united in its
hatred of him. Her own personal life is in crisis, and
she finds her path increasingly intersecting with that
of chief witness, Ellen O'Neil . . .

Pandora Women Crime Writers
LC8 232pp
Paperback: 0–86358–200–1

Also available from Pandora Press

Contemporary Crime

Amateur City *Katherine V Forrest*	£3.95 ☐
Fieldwork *Maureen Moore*	£3.95 ☐
The Monarchs are Flying *Marion Foster*	£3.95 ☐
Murder at the Nightwood Bar *Katherine V Forrest*	£3.95 ☐
Something Shady *Sarah Dreher*	£4.95 ☐
Stoner McTavish *Sarah Dreher*	£4.95 ☐
Study in Lilac *Maria Antonia Oliver*	£3.95 ☐
Vanishing Act *Joy Magezis*	£4.95 ☐
Victims *Shirley Shea*	£3.95 ☐

Classic Crime

Blood Upon the Snow *Hilda Lawrence*	£3.95 ☐
Bring the Monkey *Miles Franklin*	£3.95 ☐
Death of a Doll *Hilda Lawrence*	£3.95 ☐
Duet of Death *Hilda Lawrence*	£3.95 ☐
Easy Prey *Josephine Bell*	£3.95 ☐
Green for Danger *Christianna Brand*	£3.95 ☐
The Hours before Dawn *Celia Fremlin*	£3.95 ☐
London Particular *Christianna Brand*	£3.95 ☐
Mischief *Charlotte Armstrong*	£3.95 ☐
Murder's Little Sister *Pamela Branch*	£3.95 ☐
Murder in Pastiche *Marion Mainwaring*	£3.95 ☐
The Port of London Murders *Josephine Bell*	£3.95 ☐
The Spinster's Secret *Anthony Gilbert* (*Lucy Malleson*)	£3.95 ☐

All these books are available at your local bookshop or can be ordered direct by post. Just tick the titles you want and fill in the form below.

Name ....

Address ....

....

....

Write to Unwin Cash Sales, PO Box 11, Falmouth, Cornwall TR10 9EN. Please enclose remittance to the value of the cover price plus:

UK: 60p for the first book plus 25p for the second book, thereafter 15p for each additional book ordered to a maximum charge of £1.90.

BFPO and EIRE: 60p for the first book plus 25p for the second book and 15p per copy for the next 7 books and thereafter 9p per book.

OVERSEAS INCLUDING EIRE: £1.25 for the first book plus 75p for the second book and 28p for each additional book.

Pandora Press reserves the right to show new retail prices on covers, which may differ from those previously advertised in the text or elsewhere. Postage rates are also subject to revision.